Tasha writes murder mysteries and espionage novels with a tinge of romance, often using a nom de plume. Her characters have strong personalities that dictate the directions that the stories take. Tasha had lived and worked in North America, Western Europe and the Balkans while affiliated with interesting people doing interesting things in interesting places. She was subsequently employed as university and college faculty. These experiences are woven into her themes and plots. When not writing, she is reading, playing chess or backgammon, and taking photographs of intriguing scenes she encounters in her travels.

Dedicated to Judy.

Tasha Dumont

GODDESS OF THE NIGHT

AUSTIN MACAULEY PUBLISHERS™

LONDON • CAMBRIDGE • NEW YORK • SHARJAH

A CIP catalogue record for this title is available from the British Library.

ISBN 9781528918220 (Paperback)
ISBN 9781528918237 (Hardback)
ISBN 9781528962230 (ePub e-book)

www.austinmacauley.com

First Published (2019)
Austin Macauley Publishers Ltd
25 Canada Square
Canary Wharf
London
E14 5LQ

Chapter 1

"Ralph, you there?" A commanding voice reverberated off the back wall of the Bayview Hotel office, which obscured direct sight of anyone seated at the solitary desk.

"I'm here," Ralph Perry glanced at the digital clock on the display console. It was ten minutes after the hour precisely. With British rail precision, Constable Susan Archer strolled into the office at the exact same time each night with a confident demeanour and a warming smile. She always appreciated the aromatic stimulation of the caffeine and the potential for intellectual conversation. You couldn't find too many people with post-secondary education working the night shifts. Ralph was the only exception Sue was aware of.

Some work nights out of choice, either because they like the relative peace and quiet or they just want to avoid plunging into the deep end of the pool of humanity. Others have displeased their bosses somehow, and as a result, have been condemned to Dante's inferno, or worse, purgatorio.

Recently, Sue had been condemned to the purgatorio of the night shift because she had annoyed her supervisor by shunning his unsolicited amorous advances. She had registered a sexual harassment complaint with her boss but it was found to be unsubstantiated due to insufficient conclusive evidence and a dearth of corroboration. That was the documented bureaucratic justification for the dismissal of her allegations.

For Ralph, it was a conscious choice to be the solitary night auditor for the Bayview Hotel. He could see professional paradise, the elusive independent LED light at the end of the intern tunnel that glowed brighter as each shift ended. It was steady employment as he worked to complete courses toward a Chartered Accountant certification.

"Any interesting personalities or unusual incidents, Ralph?" Sue asked. Her tone tended to teeter between interrogation and titillating inquisition with a smattering of the jovial.

"Just the usual."

"That makes my life easy because I can just cut and paste the details from last night's report into tonight's. Even the weather is the same."

"Where's your new partner?"

"He's in the car running some plates. He's very focused on detail and analysis, so should become a good investigator if he can survive the bullshit that rains down from on high. Speaking of which, here he comes now."

Sue's new partner was the perfect poster boy for RCMP recruiting. At six feet two inches, one hundred and ninety pounds of solid physique, and Hollywood handsomeness replete with a square jaw, he would be a magnet for potential recruits to sign on the dotted line. His only challenge, given his commanding stature, was an easy entrance and quick exit from the mid-sized patrol cars.

If push came to shove, Sue had a reputation of being able to punch at her height and weight, which was a confident five foot eight and one hundred and fifty pounds. She had toned up lately, pumping iron in training for her black belt judo competition. A few of the more hubris locals might continue to question Sue's authoritative directions, despite her prowess, commanding presence and reputation for standing her ground, but would have second thoughts with her new partner by her side.

"Ralph, this is my partner in crime fighting, Constable Ben McLeod. Ben, meet Ralph, the night auditor at the hotel."

"Nice to meet you, Ben. Are you from BC or are you an import to the west coast?"

"Good to meet you too, Ralph. Right the first time. I'm a BC boy, born and raised in Trail. Moved to Victoria where I recently completed a BA in Spanish and Cultural

8

Anthropology at the University of Victoria. Joined the Force about eight months ago. This is my first posting and night shift."

"Welcome to Lotus Land," Ralph acknowledged with a gracious bow. "At least working nights, you'll have the days off to cruise the area. There is something aesthetically pleasing about a summer's day on the beaches."

Ben smiled with an acknowledgement of the tacit reference to the inviting beach scenery.

"Have you always wanted to be a police officer?"

"Growing up, I read all of the Sherlock Holmes mystery novels by Sir Arthur Conan Doyle. That pretty well defined my career path. What about you?"

"Numbers seemed to come naturally to me. I excelled in the maths and finance courses in high school. Like Sherlock Holmes, pragmatic deductive reasoning appealed to me. It was an easy choice."

"Sue told me that you always have a fresh brew of java beans on for the weary travellers and relatively palatable donuts to boot."

"*A votre plaisir, monsieur.* A parade of luminaries meander into the hotel lobby attracted by the aroma of the simmering coffee brewed with the beans that Juan Valdez had swept off the table onto the floor. In addition, I offer a limited yet selected array of succulent day-old donuts for those needing a late-night cholesterol fix but not willing or able to afford first editions off the baker's assembly line. The owner of King's Bakery, Joan Kerr, donates them to my cause in exchange for complementary financial advice, and help with her personal and business income tax returns."

"Sounds like a fair exchange."

What Ralph didn't divulge was the fact that Joan also passed along titbits of information or just plain unglazed gossip that some of her shadier customers had furtively divulged in exchange for a complimentary second cup that they falsely assumed would accelerate their sobriety. Ralph then relayed selective intelligence that he had vetted for accuracy to the local constabulary in return for extra patrols of the hotel property. The barter economy worked well.

"I didn't catch your last name, Ralph."

"Perry. Ralph Perry. Not a really exciting name but it suits the appeal of the vocation."

"Thanks. Sue also said that you have a regular parade of short-term clients in the parking lot, and occasionally in a select few rooms that are rented out by the hour, fragranced with the air of stale tobacco and bargain-basement perfume."

"Oh, yeah. They keep me entertained into the wee small hours of the night. I only wish that they wouldn't decorate the lot with a sorted array of select clothing, wine bottles and beer cans when cop cars stealthily cruise onto the asphalt like imperceptible fog off the water catching the unwary and otherwise preoccupied off guard."

"Speaking of cans, can I ask a favour of you?"

"Sure, Ben. What?"

"Can you keep a record of the makes and models, and the times, and what the occupants leave behind? I'm doing some anthropological research on what people discard, artefacts that are left for the jaws of the dumpsters."

"Yeah, OK. It'll actually break the boredom of the night a bit more. I have a couple of regulars. One is a dark blue Ford that tends not to leave anything behind, except cigarette butts. Haven't seen it this evening though. Another regular is a white Toyota that pretty consistently leaves in its wake decorative exotic lingerie with thrift store tags still attached, and screw-on cap plastic contoured wine bottles. Neither the apparel nor the nectar of the vines is of exquisite quality. Of course, I can only speak with any level of confidence to the wine and not the evening attire. You just missed the Toyota by about five minutes."

Ben chuckled as he winked at his new partner.

"I still have some samples from yesterday morning in the garbage. Wanna sift through it?"

"No thanks." Ben's smile seemed to extend from ear to ear, and was accompanied with lofty baritone laughter. "But most grateful for the gracious offer nonetheless."

"Hate to break up this intellectual conversation, guys. Ralph, have you seen Glenda lately? She's usually working Lower Main Street by now. I haven't seen her all evening and neither has anyone else. I'm not overly concerned right now but would be much happier if I could account for all the regulars."

"The last time I saw Glen was Monday afternoon. Ho Chen, the hotel owner, had asked me to come in early to answer some questions that Glen had about the hotel's books. He was preparing a response to an inquiry by Canada Revenue Agency."

"Who's Glen? I was asking about Glenda," Sue interjected.

"Glen is Glenda, or didn't you know?"

"Ah … no," Sue admitted with a subdued expression of speculation. Not much fazed her. But on occasion, she would cock her head slightly to the right and with widened eyes, raised eyebrows and a sheepish grin, shoot a surprised look. This was one of those times.

"By day, Glen is an accountant with Coast Accounting. He does the books for the hotel. He's been one of my mentors as of late, helping me with my accounting degree program. Very knowledgeable! By night, he or she is Glenda the drag queen. On occasion, he takes off for a few days on what he calls business trips."

Sue was not a naïve twenty-year-old learning about the facts of life for the first time. Wrinkles covered by her foundation makeup and grey roots disguised by her hair colouring masked the overt manifestations of some rough years accentuated by physical and mental abuse at the hands of her ex. She had joined the Mounted Police on the heels of her divorce five years ago, motivated as much by the need to break away from her previous subservient abusive life accented with infidelity as by her aspiration for financial stability and independence.

"Don't look too amazed, Sue. Welcome to the night shift. It comes with the territory."

"Not so much amazed as constantly intrigued. Sometimes I think that I've heard it all. Then I get reminded that the more I think that I know, the more I know that I don't know."

Ben took a discrete short step backward. His affable smile was replaced with an expression of muted amusement. He acknowledged the context of the implications of the discussion with a raising of his bushy dark eyebrows. Trail was also known for its home-grown luminaries.

Chapter 2

As they exited the hotel parking lot and set course for the downtown, Ben caught sight of a dark blue Ford as it slid in behind them at what appeared to be a safe distance.

"Do you recognise a dark coloured Ford Crown Victoria?" Ben asked as he monitored the rear-view mirror.

"Why do you ask?"

"Since we left Ralph's day-old donut and coffee, one has been following us at a safe distance."

"Pull over and see what it does," Sue directed with a forceful voice that left little for individual interpretation.

Ben slid to a stop and both watched through the rear-view mirrors the other vehicle do the same.

"I'm going to turn around and back track." As Ben started his manoeuvre, the other car turned right and sped away at an accelerating rate.

"Follow and see if you can catch up," Sue instructed in an even more commanding anxious tone. But by the time they reached the intersection, the suspect vehicle was nowhere in sight.

"Asshole," she muttered under her breath.

"I gather that you recognise the vehicle."

"Maybe. Take your next left and your first right after that."

"On it, partner. Where are we heading?"

As they turned right, Sue uttered in distain, "pull up alongside the dark blue Crown Victoria and stop."

As he did, Sue stepped out and placed her hand on the hood and under the front wheel. "Just as I thought. That asshole."

Ben queried with a stronger response. "Who owns the car, Sue?"

"He just stopped and took off on foot. I can smell the familiar fumes coming off the engine. If he wasn't in such a rush, he'd have parked under his condo which has a secure garage door, but he didn't have time."

"Who, Sue?" Ben demanded in a louder frustrated voice augmented with a direct stare at his partner who, for whatever reason, seemed to be evading the reply to his repeated question.

"Corporal Bill Kaplanski."

"Your previous supervisor?" Ben quizzed for clarification.

"Yes, one in the same. Ever since I filed the sexual harassment complaint against him and he beat the charges, he's been following me. I'm convinced that he thinks that he can do anything he wants. I got moved to the night shift while he stayed on days. The shift rotates but he can now harass me in his own car when he's on the opposite watch. That's what they call separating the complainant from the respondent. Let's get out of here."

As they turned back onto Lower Main Street and headed to the waterfront, the morning light began to seep onto the horizon.

"Let's complete one last circuit before calling it quits for the night," Sue uttered with an irritated growl.

The night shift report would be same old, same old, cut and paste from the previous night. They wouldn't mention Kaplanski's antics despite the fact that it was an ongoing occurrence. Sue was more troubled at her inability to stop Kaplanski from harassing her than anything else. She could feel the rising tension in her fists that were clenched in a tight boxer's grip.

"What's that?" Sue barked out.

"Where? What?"

"Back up. In the alley."

The spotlight mounted on the side of the patrol car put the depressing bleak reality into sharper focus. Protruding from behind a garbage bin at an awkward angle were two legs covered in torn mesh nylons. Ben turned the car off at the entrance to an alley as his partner bolted from her seat. Within seconds, he had joined her. They stood in stunned silence. Both beams of their flashlights simultaneously stopped on the bloodied contorted face and mangled neck of a lifeless soul. The smeared makeup suggested that it possibly was or had once been a youthful female looking as helpless in death as she was in life. A jagged gash extended the length of her corrugated neck. The left carotid artery had been brutally severed. What remained of the clothes on the upper torso were sodden with fresh crimson blood that had discoloured her splayed blond hair. Sue bent down and gingerly touched the side of the neck that had not been sliced open to check for a pulse. There was none. The body was warm. The crime scene was fresh. The sweet pungent smell of death had not fully ascended.

There were only a few circumstances that gave Sue pause. Stumbling onto a brutal murder scene was one of them. She knew interpersonal violence all too well from her own dysfunctional family and malevolent marriage. These shards of memory, both ancient and recent, would not reduce her resolve for professionalism.

"Call it in, Ben. Cover me while I check to see if anyone is hiding in the alley. Secure this entrance to the alley."

With pistol drawn and the aim illuminated with the projected beam of the flashlight held in her other hand that also steadied her grip, she commenced the methodical search of the walled proximity to the scene. Ben had her back with a parallel offensive stance. There was only one way out and he had it covered.

The alley barely extended twenty metres from Lower Main Street to the back-brick wall that had been scrawled with multiple layers of indecipherable graffiti. The alley was used for deliveries to adjacent businesses and extrication of trash. Sue called back to her partner after searching inside and around garbage containers, and carefully checking doors to ensure that they were secure. "All clear!"

"Backup, Ident and Major Crime are en route, Sue. Dog Master is also on the way. Where it's this fresh, we might get lucky with a fresh scent. We're to remain on scene until the dayshift NCO relieves us."

"Good call on the Dog Master, partner."

As they finished securing the familiar yellow crime scene tape across the entrance to the alley, Sue directed Ben to conduct a cursory check of the sidewalk to the left of the entrance for one block, back across the street, then back to the ally on the right. She stood sentinel at the tape and scanned the panorama for any suspicious sounds or movement, all along maintaining continuity of the scene and visual contact with her partner.

The body didn't look like Glenda but there was too much smeared blood mixed with mascara and dishevelled hair to get an accurate identification. There were other possibilities. One was a transvestite whose physical characteristics were similar to Glenda's, Glen's. She was one of many of the others belonging to the breed of lost souls known as winos and druggies and homeless. "So much for a routine night shift," she muttered to herself.

Flashing blue and red lights silently announced the arrival of backup as Ben completed his hasty scan.

"Didn't see anything unusual," he reported with a sense of attuned urgency in his voice. "With backup here, I'd like to conduct a second more detailed search of the sidewalks to make sure that I didn't miss anything."

"Good plan. Go ahead. I'll have the backup seal off both ends of the street. This is all commercial so no one should be able to enter from either end. Hopefully the dog will pick up a fresh scent."

Corporal Denis Andrews and Constable Erin Johnson from Ident were on-scene within minutes. Sue crisply provided a briefing and turned the crime scene over to them. She recorded the time and date of the hand-over in her notebook and received a verbal confirmation of the change in continuity.

"Excellent job, Sue," Denis commented, "You should be teaching how to secure a crime scene to all field officers. You've certainly made our job easier on this case. I'll mention it in my report."

Denis was aware of Sue's harassment complaint and the disappointing outcome, as was everyone else in the detachment. He was also acutely aware of Kaplanski's reputation for such unprofessional antics. After all these years, there were still dinosaurs in the upper echelons of the organisation.

If discovering the grisly body wasn't stressful enough, Corporal Kaplanski unexpectedly confronted Sue. He had just arrived looking and smelling like he recently rolled out of the drunk tank.

"What are you doing here?" Sue growled at him in an accusatory manner as she glared at his dark blue Crown Victoria and took a whiff of the all too familiar engine fumes floating from the wheel wells. She sensed Ben's close proximity and was surprised at the reassurance that she felt.

"I heard your call on the radio scanned in my car."

"And ... So," Sue gruffly rebuffed in an unmistakeable strident voice, all along asking herself why he had a police scanner in his own car. There could only be one reason and she didn't like it any more than she appreciated his presence at this scene.

"Do you need any assistance?" Kaplanski asked in an almost guilty tone.

"No. Why would I? I've turned the scene over to Corporal Andrews, who I doubt will be happy with you contaminating the crime scene. I'm about to return to the office to file my report, which I can complete by myself."

"Kaplanski!" Andrews yelled. "What the hell are you doing here messing with my crime scene? Get out of here and take your stinking personal car with you. You'll be hearing about your bad judgement from the Detachment Commander. Sue knows more about securing a crime scene than you ever will."

Like a scolded mangy mongrel, Kaplanski sullenly returned to his car and departed the scene. Denis shot Sue a confident glance and a self-assured subtle smile.

As Ben got back in their patrol car, he heard Sue mutter under her breath, "What a creep."

"My sentiment exactly." His warm supportive smile brought a bolstered reassurance to her. She thought for a moment that there was something of an honourable heraldic knight in his manner. If push came to shove, she had no doubt that he would be there for her.

"And by the way, thanks for backing me up with your close proximity when Kaplanski approached me."

"Any time, partner, any time."

***

Sue and Ben had been relieved within an hour of discovering the gruesome corpse. It wasn't a common occurrence at the detachment. Sue had previously only seen one criminal cadaver and that was at an autopsy. This was Ben's first which put him ahead of many who had retired with no such stories to embellish for their grandchildren.

The police dog, Riley, had followed a scent from the body out of the alley and right along Lower Main Street to the first intersection where the trail went cold. Corporal Lynn Duval, the Dog Master, figured that the assailant had left a get-away car at the intersection, or had been picked up by an accomplice who had knowingly abetted in the offence.

Major Crime from Sub-Division had arrived before Sue and Ben had completed the paper work, including overtime claims that were not acknowledged with the same enthusiasm but instead with spurned scrutiny.

Chapter 3

"Good afternoon, Ben. I see that you're taking in the aesthetically pleasing mid-afternoon beach panorama."

"I'd say the same to you, Ralph."

"I heard through the grape vine that your shift wasn't a cut and paste routine."

"News travels fast."

"Was it Glenda or Glen?"

"Don't know Ralph, and couldn't say if I did know."

"I appreciate that. Hopefully the identity of the victim will be released before you and Sue drop by for java tonight."

"I could contact you earlier in exchange for a little intel."

"I like your style, Ben. How can I assist you?"

"Last evening, you mentioned that one of the regulars to your parking lot was a dark blue Ford."

"Yes."

"Would that be a dark blue Ford Crown Victoria by chance?"

"By chance, you are in luck. In fact, it seemed to pull in behind you after you left my coffee beans last night. It might have been just serendipitous but I had a feeling that it was following you."

"If you see it again tonight in your parking lot, can you make note of the licence plate and perhaps get a glimpse of the driver?"

"Could do. Is it connected to the murder investigation? Do I need to be cautious, Ben?"

"No, it's not connected. It's a sensitive personal matter involving Sue. I wouldn't want you to mention to her that we chatted about this."

A hiatus followed before Ben re-engaged with his guarded enquiry. "It has to do with an administrative matter. An in-house issue that Sue initiated."

"Her harassment case?" Ralph replied with a tone of inquisitiveness.

"News does travel fast," Ben confirmed.

"I have a great deal of respect for Sue. How can I help?" Ralph offered.

"Corporal Kaplanski has been harassing Sue. I'm pretty sure that he was following us last night. He drives a dark blue Ford Crown Victoria. It would sure be nice to put a crimp in his nocturnal marauding."

"Consider it done, Ben. Anything to help, just ask. I'd be honoured to serve some of those who serve."

Ben projected his Hollywood smile. "In the immortal words of one of my silver screen heroes, 'Louis, I think this is the beginning of a beautiful friendship'."

"Bogie. Casablanca. 1942! One of my favourite classic Hollywood heroes also," Ralph jubilantly uttered with equal adoration for Humphrey Bogart.

***

"Bayview Hotel. How may I help you?"

"Ralph, it's Ben. The deceased is not Glen or Glenda, but one of Sue's regulars, a tranny who's been heavy into drugs. The name will be released once the next of kin have been notified. Have to go. Sue is calling me."

"Much appreciated, Ben. Java beans await the weary wary travellers."

No sooner had Ralph hung up, when the familiar dark blue Ford Crown Victoria passed by the flood lit canopy at the front entrance to the parking lot, and silently slid into a secluded shadowed vacant stall. Ralph waited for an appropriate time for the occupants to embark in non-verbal discourse before silently approaching from an angle that would not be readily detected. He noted the licence number. Although his view of the interior was partially obscured by the quasi-opaque humidity forming on the interior of the glass, it was readily apparent that the occupants were otherwise engaged. The driver's door suddenly opened as Ralph abruptly rapped on the window.

"What the hell do you want?" the driver demanded sharply as he hastily stepped out all the while attempting to obscure Ralph's view of the passenger. Anticipating his manoeuvre, Ralph adeptly added an additional iPhoto to his iCloud album.

"I work here. I don't mind you parking in the lot but would very much appreciate you not discarding trash," Ralph replied with a sense of conviction.

"I don't litter or pollute," the driver barked. "What's with the photo?"

"Corporal Kaplanski?" Ralph re-engaged sarcastically.

"You must be mistaken."

"No. I've seen you in the detachment."

"Can we keep this between us?" Kaplanski muttered under his breath that reeked of stale virtues of the vine. "I can do you favours if you don't mention this."

"Well, that makes all the difference in the world, Corporal Kaplanski. I do have one demand."

"Demand! Who the hell do you think you are demanding anything of me?" Kaplanski retorted with a pretentious arrogant air of superiority.

Ralph held up his cell phone. "I can always email the pic which I just took and our conversation that I just recorded to the Detachment Commander."

Kaplanski's face turned as beet red as the scarlet tunic of his dress uniform. "What do you want?"

"Now that's better," Ralph replied in a conciliatory negotiating tone. "Let's step to the back of your vehicle, out of ear shot of your lady friend."

Kaplanski followed like an admonished puppy caught after defiantly defecating on a prized Persian carpet.

Again holding up his cell phone, Ralph stated unequivocally. "You avoid Sue Archer. If I hear that you are following her or calling her or doing anything that might be construed as harassment as defined by the RCMP, or even a dirty rumour that you are anywhere near her, I will forward the pic and the recording to the Commissioner in Ottawa, the Commanding Officer of E Division in Vancouver and your Detachment Commander. Have I made myself perfectly clear, Corporal Kaplanski?"

As Ralph laid out his demands, Kaplanski automatically came to attention, as if being called to account for a perfidious indiscretion by his recruit training drill staff.

"Yes, sir." Kaplanski obediently uttered.

"Carry on, Corporal. You are dismissed," Ralph directed in his best authoritative, corporate auditing voice. He turned around and traipsed back to the hotel office leaving Kaplanski to recompose himself. All the while inwardly smiling.

Ben's cell phone hummed. The text message read, 'There should not be any re-occurrences. But if there are, let me know.' It was signed: 'Bogie.'

"All OK," Sue enquired.

"All OK."

Chapter 4

"Ralph, you there?"

"I'm here, Sue. I understand that your shift wasn't as uneventful as you thought it would be after you left last night."

"It's the old adage of be careful what you ask for because you just might get it. I was thinking about a little less mundane shift and got considerably more."

"Any word on the identity of the victim?"

"I can tell you that it wasn't Glenda or Glen. It was one of my other regulars. Her name will be released once the next of kin have been notified."

"That's good to hear that it wasn't Glen. But very unfortunate that anyone has to end their life under such gruesome circumstances."

"It's weird, Ralph. The Major Crime investigators seemed to know that it wasn't Glen without any confirmed ID. It was as if they knew or knew of Glen. My intuition is telling me that something else, some skulduggery of sorts, is at play beyond our sleepy hollow, possibly with an Ichabod Crane association. I'm sensing even with a possible international connection. Are you hearing anything on your end?"

"Haven't noticed any headless horsemen wandering into the parking lot. But now that you ask, when I picked up the day-old donuts at King's Bakery, Joan mentioned that the murder was drug related. Word has it that the victim was scamming on the side, trying to pull a fast one on her supplier, her John. The murder was purposely vicious as a lesson. Another supplier may be trying to move in and may have ensnared the deceased to transfer allegiances. She paid the price for her reluctance."

The thought of a drug war on her turf assailed Sue like the worst-case scenario of Ebenezer Scrooge's ghost of Christmas past. The law of unintended consequences of such a battle space within her relatively quiet community was not an option she wanted to contemplate but one that she had to consider carefully. On the west coast, the reality of escalation of drug activity was harrowing. It had both regional and global consequences. Sue became fixed on the image of the brutality of a single blood drenched body in a back alley multiplied tenfold or one hundred fold.

"Are you thinking what I'm thinking?" Ben queried.

"Sub Division Drug folks have been focused on the north west coast of the Island more recently. Apparently, one of the cartels out of Central America, with a Mayan connection, has been active cultivating potential business partners. The west side of the Island has become too hot, so they may be looking for new, untapped and fertile markets on the east side, on our generative turf."

After a pensive pause, Ben huffed, "The plot thickens."

Sue was beginning to read her partner's subtle innuendoes as expressions of his contemplative processing. "The plot thickens," Sue echoed.

"One of the more mature students from my degree program at UVic was from Cancun on the Yucatan peninsula. She never really told me that much about her background. But I got the feeling that she may have been involved in the drug trade somehow, either on the periphery of trafficking or enforcement, or perhaps both as an informant. She came to Victoria as much to further her education, as to put some distance between herself and a few personalities in Cancun, to get out of Dodge and away from the corrupt sheriff, per se. She had a keen interest in anthropology and talked a lot about her Mayan culture and specifically the Mayan ruins at San Gervasio. We've kept in contact although I don't think that I ever told her what I do. Let me send her an email and snoop around a bit."

"OK. But be careful. These cartel folks can be ruthless when it comes to anyone encroaching into their territory or adversely impacting their bottom line."

"Very much appreciate that. Thanks for the heads up."

"Would you mind sharing her name, just in case things go sideways on this? My instinct is sending me warning signals. I've learned that my intuition is never wrong. It's just my misconception of my intuition that gets me into trouble."

"No problem. Her name is Alejandra Martinez. When last we exchanged emails, she was in Gibsons or Sechelt. She mentioned that she really liked the remoteness and seclusion of that part of the Sunshine Coast and the off-the-beaten-path laid back lifestyle, especially Roberts Creek and Davis Bay hamlets. There's a story there with intrigue. I just don't have all the details, at least not yet."

"OK. But let's first chat with our local clientele, just as a matter of routine. We won't overdo it and spook them. One of the shadowy ladies is a confidential informant of mine. I'll contact her privately. It's not that I don't trust you, Ben, it's just that she gets skittish around others. It's the law of the jungle, being extra wary."

"How easy would it be to get a confidence payment for Alejandra if it pans out that she can provide us with nourishing morsels of intel?"

"Normally, not a big deal. There's a procedure to follow. I can walk you through that process."

"What about an informant?"

"If you believe that it would be worthwhile to turn her into a paid informant, the formal procedure is more involved. It would be considerably more difficult in this specific case if there were tentacles into the international arena with drug implications. The drug guys from Sub Division are exceedingly jealous and tenaciously protective of what they perceive to be their turf. Anyone who busted this case, if there are international repercussions, would earn great accolades from on high. As you know, promotion is based more on individual merit than on team performance. The drug section would not want to share the spotlight with a junior probationary constable and a female member who has challenged the Force with a harassment allegation. I wonder sometimes who's on whose side. Let's take it one step at a time so we don't inadvertently step on anyone's delicate toes."

"Politics," Ben chuckled.

"More like minefields," Sue suggested.

Ben seemed to withdraw from the conversation as he took a series of deep, slow, silent breaths.

After an interlude of reflection, Sue quietly enquired, "Wanna talk about it?" The temptation to second-guess her partner was present, but she resisted in favour of an introspective pause and an open opportunity for Ben to re-engage. She swallowed her judgements, sensing that something had touched a nerve, which ran deep. She recognised all too well the symptoms, the manifestations of shards of painful memories of abuse and violence from her own past.

"While living in Trail, I worked part-time with the Field Engineers, an Army Reserve Unit. I served with the Canadian military on a mission in Afghanistan. One of my buddies was blown up while attempting to remove the fuse from a landmine. So when you said that politics was more like a minefield, I thought about my friend."

A solemn moment passed. It was Sue's turn to ruminate in silence. "Yikes! Sorry about that. I didn't know. You don't wear the campaign ribbon on your uniform."

"Not your fault, Sue. You wouldn't have known. Most of the time, it's just a vexing memory on the shelf. Once in a while, the memory falls off the shelf and bonks me on the head. I just put it back on the shelf, rub my head, and get on with things. In engineering lingua, build a bridge and get over it. Shit happens sometimes. Yeah, I don't wear the Afghanistan ribbon, as you say, because some days it is just too heavy to wear and bear."

"Good to know, partner. Thanks for sharing that."

"Let's get back on the case." Ben re-joined the analysis with greater levity in his demeanour. "We have a murder to solve before the Sub-Division Major Crime folks, and some international drug lords to catch before the Sub-Division Drug Section guys and gals. I do like a competitive challenge."

"You realise that if we solve these cases, we'll have to buy some matching black-rimmed sun glasses, like the Blues Brothers, to deflect the sparkle from the spotlights of Hollywood North tinsel town that will be on us. The Legend of Sleepy Hollow will have to be rewritten with an altered cast of characters."

Ben confidently chuckled. "Not if, partner, but when?"

There was something in the way he spoke, in his manner, that suggested that there was no doubt. They would solve the cases. It was a *fait accompli*. He had ambition but wasn't excessively ambitious. It would be a mistake to confuse his confidence with arrogance. Ben may have been from a small community but his perspective and potential were convincingly metropolitan.

Chapter 5

"Anderson's Accounting, how may I help you?"

"Could I speak with Glen?"

"He's out of the office at the moment, but expected back late this afternoon. Would you like to leave a voice mail?"

"It's Ralph Perry. Could you have him call me as soon as he gets in?"

"I can do that Ralph. He called me this morning saying that he had been unavoidably delayed. His meeting with Canada Revenue Agency on the Bayview Hotel file was taking longer than expected."

"Thanks, Anne. Take care."

Ralph reflected on Sue's previous observation that Glen had been eliminated almost off hand as the potential murder victim by the Major Crime investigators. CRA had sent Ho a form letter stating that there were no outstanding taxation issues. Why would Glen be meeting with them about the hotel and why would a meeting be taking up so much time? Ralph's subjective intuition was challenging his accountant modus operandi of objectivity. The purported words of another of his silver screen Hollywood hero rang clear, 'Just the facts, Ma'am.' Ralph was no Detective Joe Friday but Dan Aykroyd who mimicked Jack Webb in the leading roll on the 1950s TV series, Dragnet, summed up his motivation at the moment. Something wasn't quite right. If it were simply an accounting transaction, he wouldn't give it a second guess. But the potential consequences had drastically turned deadly. He needed to have a tête-à-tête with Ben and possibly Sue.

'Chat time?' was the pithy text title that appeared on Ben's cell.

Ben tapped the keyboard in rapid response. 'At the beach. Loc?'

'Be there in 10' appeared on his display before he could sip his coffee.

Ben greeted his new comrade with an affable grin and his best Bugs Bunny adaption, "Ah, what's up doc?"

"I'm thinking that there is mutual benefit in combining forces. Excuse the pun," Ralph proposed.

"I'm all ears, if you excuse my Bugs Bunny pun. What do you have in mind?"

"Last night, Sue mentioned that she felt that something wasn't right with the initial response by the Major Crime investigators to the immediate elimination of Glen or Glenda as the murder victim. I just spoke with Glen's admin assistant. He is very much alive and will be back in his office this afternoon. Supposedly, he has been meeting with CRA on a file that has been closed. There have been some other inconsistencies recently, a few with connections to your colleagues in Commercial Crime and possibly a related narcotic investigation. I agree with Sue's assessment. Something isn't right. If it was just white-collar crime stuff, I might be intrigued but certainly wouldn't be perturbed. But I'm getting the impression that it's mixed in with the murder, and that's beyond bothersome. Murder and drugs are a volatile cocktail."

Ben scanned the beach scenery, all the while looking without really seeing. "Sue and I shared similar feelings, more so Sue. I'm thinking that we need to bring Sue into the conversation because of the severity of the potentially ominous consequences. There are some seriously bad actors out there."

Ralph nodded in concurrence. "I'm OK with that."

"I have the quasi protection of a badge and a gun, and an organisation with a reputation for backroom retribution, although lately I have been questioning the integrity of that eroding repute. You don't have the inauspicious safeguards of the red coats when they defiantly close ranks against any potential external threat. It has become abundantly clear in my brief service that the Force may eat their young behind closed doors, but they are merciless like a pack of jackals in their relentless retaliation against anyone who takes on an individual member. It's not a threat. It's not a promise. It's just an irrefutable fact."

"I don't want to appear as paranoid, but perhaps we should meet in less public places. Prudence if not providence is appropriate."

"I'm quickly coming to the same ardent conclusion," Ben affirmed. "How about we strategise further tonight when Sue and I stop by for our routine fix of caffeine and day-old cholesterol."

"Look forward to it. By then, hopefully I'll have met with Glen and should have an update on his activities or at least my intuitive assessment of his dubious comings and goings. In the interim, I'll chat with Ho and see if I can pick up anything. He could be involved directly or on the periphery."

"10-4. I'll snoop around with some of my colleagues also." Ben added. "I can play the part of the dumb probie junior constable innocently demonstrating naïve initiative in an attempt to learn the ropes. Sherlock Holmes theorises that the more you probe the beast, the better you understand its phobias, its strengths and weaknesses."

"You sound like you're a graduate of psychology, not anthropology."

Ben retorted with his familiar baritone chuckle. "Anthropology is culture as is the psyche of the people. The more perspectives you employ to analyse a phenomenon, the greater will be your understanding of what makes it tick. That's why I did a double major in Spanish and Cultural Anthropology. The Spanish language speaks to the psychology of the Mayan culture and its Spanish ancestries."

"*Jusqu'à ce soir, mon ami*, until tonight, my friend." Ralph concluded with a leisurely bow and a languid adieu.

Chapter 6

"Ralph, its Glen. You called. How can I help?"

"Thanks for returning my call. Anne mentioned that you were working with CRA on the Bayview Hotel file. I thought that it was closed. Am I missing something?"

"No. Bayview is concluded. My meeting had to do with another file of a supplier. Nothing important."

Ralph sensed an apprehension in Glen's terse response. "OK. Thanks. The reason I asked, I'm working on a final case study for one of my auditing courses. I appreciate the confidentiality. As always, anything you can share would be of help."

"I'll drop by the hotel in a couple of days. We can chat then. Need to get caught up on some other files first."

***

"One of these nights, Sue, you are not going to arrive exactly on time and I'm going to become anxious that something bad has happened," Ralph uttered as he poured two cups of coffee for his nocturnal guests.

"You worry more about me than my supervisor, Ralph. But I welcome your caring and concern. With Ben riding shotgun, you can rest assured that I'll be safe. Ben briefed me on your conversation this afternoon. I agree that there would be mutual benefit in us sharing intel."

As they wended their way to the back office, Ben checked an incoming email. Alejandra had replied positively to his request to get together. She mentioned that they could meet at a café south of Sechelt, where she was working as a baker. He was to ask for Marcelle Santos. Given what he knew about her background, he wasn't all that surprised with her request. She had taken pains to be normal but normality had long since eluded her. A shadow of sadness momentarily passed over him as he reflected on what he remembered of the imprecise often-fleeting stories regarding her entangled life in the Yucatan peninsula.

"Just to let you know, Ralph, Ben and I are off for the next two days. Don't want you worrying that something may have happened. I'll send you my personal, confidential email in the event that something major rears its ugly head. Please don't give it to anyone."

"Thanks, Sue. I'll honour the confidentiality request."

"Ben mentioned that you agree with my concern that something just doesn't seem right with regards to what has transpired amongst my colleagues about the murder investigation."

"I spoke with Glen late this afternoon. I got the sense that he wasn't telling me the truth, the whole truth and nothing but the truth. I also spoke with Ho who said that CRA had recommended Glen to be the accountant for the hotel. CRA supposedly assured Ho that his tax returns would receive favourable review if Glen's signature was on the covering letter. That is highly irregular to say the least. Thinking back to when we first met, Glen approached me and strongly offered to mentor me. It's not uncommon for a business accountant like Glen to introduce himself to the bookkeeper as a potential protégé, but there seemed to be a hidden agenda or alternate motive. I'm not a psychologist but Glen is too strait-laced to be a drag queen by night. An accountant, yes, but not a lady of the night."

Sue drew her eyebrows together and shifted her gaze upward in deliberation before responding. "I've never met Glen. Maybe I should to get a take on him. It's not that I don't trust you, Ralph, it's just that the stakes are high and rising."

"He said that he was going to drop by in a couple of days. I can confirm a meeting time with him and have you unexpectedly drop by."

Sue paused a bit longer. "Plan A, a chance meeting, is good. Plan B, I'll drop by his office to inquire if he could do my personal income tax return."

"I can be with you for either Plan A or Plan B," Ben offered. "In the interim, I'll be meeting with a friend who may be able to shed some light on the case."

"OK. I'll send both of you an email with the meeting time," Ralph confirmed, "*Jusqu'à ce que, mes camarades*, until then, comrades."

Chapter 7

"Funky place," Ben commented to the server standing behind the weathered wooden counter in the café. She would be second, possibly third generation hippie he guessed. Judging the age of females older than himself had always plagued him. Perhaps it was a male gender thing. Her vibrant coloured retro floral blouse and freely flowing embroidered Boho skirt complemented the late 60s and early 70s art décor.

Alejandra quietly made her entrance from the kitchen, as he was about to order his green tea and freshly baked muffin. The fleeting though of Alejandra being the culinary artist of his muffin warmed his soul.

"I'll get this," Alejandra politely whispered to the server. Her delicate glance caught Ben's.

He stood in silence and gazed with anticipation at his classmate whose appearance had changed. He winked quickly as she closed the distance. There was reserved passion in his eyes, yet he hid his emotion for the moment as he tried to read her face.

"I'll be on a break," Alejandra announced.

The other server acknowledged her with a cordial nod and affable smile as Alejandra and Ben exited the café.

They strolled down the slight incline of the road to the oceanside pier. Alejandra surreptitiously reached for his hand when out of sight of her colleagues in the café. Once on the secluded pebbled beach, she then embraced him in a manner that went beyond what would be customary of school chums.

"I've missed you, Ben," she whispered as she kissed him on the cheek, all the while tightening her hug. "God, you're looking good. You always took pride in your appearance." What she didn't relate was her thoughts and dreams that often returned to those times when they studied together and on other more personal less academic occasions.

Ben deliberated, as he would when sipping Cognac, savouring the myriad of delicate virtues. The ambience touched a chord as the melding of her accent and intoning continued to seduce him as it had done several months before.

"I've missed you too," he replied as he held her closer for a prolonged moment. Their cuddle was mutual and seemed natural. His question broke the silence.

"Tell me about the name change and grey frizzed hair. I sense that you want to remain as elusive as some aspects of the lost Mayan culture." He detected that her motivation to flee to the Sunshine Coast and change her name and appearance were as much to divest herself from the lethal baggage of her past as not to accumulate more.

Alejandra reiterated details of her past, some of which she had previously shared with him. Other specifics were new and heart wrenching. The memory of past circumstances made her voice fall and her lips quiver.

In a soft compassionate tone, he validated her honest accounts of abuse, which she related not so much as a come-to-Jesus confession but as a reckoning with her past that she wanted to share, and a genuine interest in rejuvenating a warmer relationship that had become distant since graduation. They walked without words.

Ben listened to the invitation of the silence. "How can I help, Alejandra?"

"You've already helped me more than you may ever know just by being a sounding board without judgement, and by being here now. But I surmise that you are seeking more than a renewed relationship, collegial or otherwise. It's my turn to ask, how can I help you?"

Ben revealed the details of his employment and the primary purpose of his renewed contact at this time. He acknowledged an alternate personal motivation to renew a closer connection, possibly platonic. He admitted that he had thought about her and the good times they shared at UVic on numerous occasions, usually when he was alone with his memories. She was special.

His request triggered recollections of events that she would have preferred to leave in the deep recesses of her mind. Her eyes seemed to search endlessly in an elliptical surveillance. He followed her scanning not knowing what he was looking for, his eyes questioning.

Her attention poised, she considered his request momentarily before responding. "Do you remember the class when you defended me? I was talking about my Mayan culture when another arrogant foreign student bluntly interrupted and accused me of not knowing what I was talking about. You instantly stood up and accused the bully in no uncertain terms that I knew more about Mayan anthropology than he would ever know. After class, I revealed to you that no one had ever come to my rescue before in such a noble manner, and if you ever needed anything you just had to ask me."

Her meticulous memory of that event astonished him. "Yes, I remember now that you mention it, but I didn't think anything of it at the time."

Undaunted by the prospects of being discovered, Alejandra conformed to his request and provided all the details he had asked for and more. He listened with rapt attentiveness as she bared her soul. Ben realised that the details revealed were ingredients of an elixir of death, certainly for Alejandra and potentially for him. He feared for her safety and contemplated how far he would go to protect her. Experiencing a convenient lapse of memory would be high on the list of options he would employ if he was pressed to identify his source.

As the significance of the information sunk in, Ben starred at her. "I won't pose the question I was thinking of asking you because I know what your answer would be, and I can't put you in the cross hairs."

She shyly smiled back at him, once again acknowledging his chivalry. "If only," she murmured, and then paused realising that now was not the occasion. Their worlds were too different, but perhaps later in another place and at another time.

"How long can you stay?" she asked with expectation of a positive response.

"Unfortunately, I need to be on the evening ferry," he lamented. *God, I could stay here forever. How could I get a transfer to Sechelt?* But deep down, he knew that such a possibility was not feasible, at least not in the short-term.

They sat on a seasoned log that had washed up on the beach pushed by waves of a winter storm, gently caressing each other's hands as the tide ebbed. Would the returning tide bring with it promising driftwood, or just peripheral seemingly extraneous flotsam and jetsam?

With a farewell embrace that lingered long and sensuous snuggling that did not linger long enough, she whispered, "I'd be open to meeting again, sooner rather than later. However, given our chosen trajectories and the severity of the matter that has brought us together today, it would have to be a very discrete rendezvous."

An enamoured ember had been rekindled with that invitation. They shared slow endearing nods and subtle sheepish yet yearning smiles at the potential prospects of such an enticing tryst. Their parting kiss sealed the sincerity of their mutual commitment to explore options for a renewed relationship, certainly sooner than later.

Chapter 8

"So how was Sechelt?" Sue asked with a tone of curiosity regarding his social life, and anticipation of intel that could help them solve the murder and gain the upper hand on the potential drug connection.

"A bit of background first," Ben pre-empted his response. "Alejandra had been and may still be a truant partner of one of the key players within the Central American drug cartel. I got the sense that she also may have slept with other equally treacherous and traitorous cartel conspirators some of whom would like to get their lecherous hands on her again. She had been very attractive once but those vestiges of youthful beauty have since been marred with scars from physical abuse. She ultimately realised that her alluring beauty could lead to her untimely demise. That was the primary motivator for her precipitous departure from the Mayan peninsula to British Columbia and the Sunshine Coast. Under her makeup, though, she could still present a fresh face and flirtatious mildness of manner. With Alejandra, you need to remember that her Mexican-Spanish modus operandi of seduction masks a mosaic of meanings. I'm not being judgemental of her. You do what you have to do to survive *en las calles* in the barrio, and she is a survivor of that subsistent vicious world."

Sue reflected on Ben's summary character analysis. However, she was compellingly drawn to his description of Alejandra's physical abuse and facial scars covered with foundation makeup. That was Sue's landmine, a reminder of the physical violence that she had endured from the fierce fists of her ex. She sensed that Ben might have been attracted to Alejandra by her beauty and vulnerability. But she was confident that he had the wherewithal not to be drawn into her seductive survival vortex. He could be there to support Alejandra, the heraldic knight, as he had been present when Kaplanski harassed her at the murder crime scene. Sue silently bemoaned the fact that Sir Ben hadn't been in her orbit when her ex was abusing her.

"Alejandra did confirm that the Mayan drug cartel is shipping cocaine to the Sunshine Coast. The primary port of entry is Sechelt, specifically Roberts Creek and Davis Bay because of its long-term reputation as a location that isn't heavily policed. The local RCMP detachment has neither a dedicated Drug Section nor a K-9 Unit. Instead, it just has a GIS. I spoke with one of the members who was a troop ahead of me at Depot. He said that policing on the Sunshine Coast is pretty laid back. The members are aware that Sechelt is a port of entry but the cocaine is quickly moved out of the region to major centres like Vancouver."

"Interesting," Sue exclaimed. "I've heard rumours to that effect. A 'don't ask, don't tell' mantra. The cocaine must be shipped out fast and not used locally. Intel that I receive suggests that there isn't a perceived need by senior executives within the Division so they don't commit resources to enforcement at this point of entry. Logic might dictate otherwise. But there seems to be another agenda, and that's what's concerning. Don't quote me on this." Sue paused as she scanned the immediate vicinity to ensure that potentially prying ears were at a safe distance. With her hand covering her mouth and blocking any possible visual interpretation, she concluded her assessment.

"You need to know, Ben, that the system is dirty. There are Members of the Force and others influential players within the judicial and political hierarchy, and the world of academia who are on the take. There is big money involved and these people will do whatever they perceive as necessary to protect their interests. So we need to be very careful, partner. Very careful."

"It's somewhat like Afghanistan," Ben validated. "Everyone looks the same on the surface. You only find out who the bad guys are when an IED blows up in front or underneath you. What's left of your mangled remains are sent home in a body bag following the ramp ceremony."

"Let's just be careful, especially when it comes to who we can trust," Sue reinforced with a wary summary.

Ben starred squarely at Sue and nodded, as much acknowledging her wariness as updating his concluding comments. "Alejandra said that some drugs are syphoned off for local use but there aren't really significant problems like a lot of deaths from overdosing. The local traffickers are aware of the need to keep a low key so as not to attract attention from drug enforcement folks or competitors in the trade. She mentioned that the traffickers tip very well when they frequent cafés and restaurants, up to two or three hundred dollars. This way, they ensure that their servers remain loyal to them. It's been a part of the local lifestyle since the 1960s when U.S. army draft dodgers moved north to the Sunshine coast. After all these years, some of these latent hippies replete with dishevelled grey-haired ponytails have become financially secure illegal aliens working in a lucrative underground economy. The barter system is alive and well."

"OK. Is Alejandra willing to provide more information, possibly become a paid informant for you?"

"I'm confident that she would provide me with more information but not become an official paid informant. She just has too much to lose, including her life. Like your local informant, she would be really skittish if you accompanied me. She'd provide me with inside information on the Mayan cartel folks but not any of her Sechelt neighbours. She emphasised the imperative for low-key anonymity. She wants to remain off the radar and we need to respect her wishes. If we're going to bust this case, and I'm confident that we can, then we need to do so without any known connection to her."

"Agreed." Sue nodded with an approved affirmation.

"Alejandra also said that the murder of the prostitute is directly connected to the Mayan drug folks. Apparently another competing cartel operating out of Guatemala is engaged in a drug war with the Mexican Mayan cartel in Belize. Whether we or the traffickers in Sechelt like it or not, war has been declared and the extended battle space is in our back yard."

Sue paused as she processed all the information that Ben had related. "Great work and good news, Ben. If we solve the murder, we might solve the drug case. Bad news, we can't just solve one without the other, and that means we really need to be strategic. At some point, we'll have to involve others, especially the Sub-Division drug folks because of the international implications. I just don't know who to trust at this juncture. First, we need to figure out a viable working relationship between you and Alejandra and how to keep her identity absolutely anonymous."

"One final point," Ben interjected. "Alejandra didn't know anything about the Bayview Hotel. When I asked about Ho Chen, she said that he wasn't involved, at least his name hadn't been mentioned or known in her circles. She'd check further and get back to me with any updates."

"That's good to know. We can mention the Bayview to Ralph but not anything else. The stakes are just too high. He still thinks that Glen or Glenda hasn't been completely forthright with him. Not being honest with a protégé isn't a crime. It may be an integrity issue. But let's not dismiss Ralph's concerns altogether, at least until we have all the facts. There may still be a connection. My intuition is telling me that there is something there that could help or hinder us."

Ben clearly heard the call to caution in Sue's voice. In the brief time they had worked together, he had seen her happy. He had seen her sad. He had seen her annoyed. He had never seen her perplexed, unsure, perhaps even a little fearful. He had learned in Afghanistan that there was always room for gracious humour especially in the severest circumstances. So, with his rehearsed sheepish grin, he posed the enduring question. "Do we buy our dark-rimmed Blues Brothers sun glasses now or later?"

Sue chuckled as she threw him a confident, comedic glance. "I like your style, partner!"

Chapter 9

Both Sue and Ben simultaneously reached for their cell phones in response to Ralph's incoming message. As usual, Glen had given his protégé his routine short fuse time appreciation. He would be at the hotel within the hour. Ralph's text concluded by encouraging his comrades to be prompt as Glen tended not to mix business with the pleasure of socialising, even with day-old donuts, which had been his Achilles heel. His expanded waistline and corresponding elevated cholesterol levels could attest to that quasi addiction.

Glen announced his arrival with his customary offer of assistance. "You mentioned that you were working on a term paper. How can I help, Ralph?"

Before his protégé could respond, Sue and Ben entered the office from the hotel lobby.

Glen paused awkwardly and lingered uneasily when he met Sue's enquiring stare. There was only one exit and that meant having to slide past Sue, and Ben whose stature left little wiggle room, which was one of Glen's favourite expressions when referring to apparent tiny loopholes in the Income Tax Act.

Ralph nonchalantly completed introductions all the while suggesting that this visitation from the constabulary was routine.

"I know you," Sue uttered while pointing her index finger at Glen.

"Don't think so," he replied abruptly. He then pulled out his cell phone and stated brusquely, "Please excuse me. I have to take this urgent confidential call." As he forced himself past Ben, Sue followed him outside into the imprecise shadows of the night.

Sue repeated, "I know you."

Again Glen denied any acquaintance.

"Yes. You're Sergeant Glen Anderson from Winnipeg Commercial Crime section. You taught me when I attended my Constable Investigation Course at the Canadian Police College in Ottawa. And, you are also known as Glenda."

Glen stopped in his tracks with that meticulous identifying pronouncement. "Come with me now, Constable Archer," he directed with a curt voice that left no question as to Sue's potential for misinterpretation of his intention or her flexibility. Glen led the way back into the office where he grabbed a key to a vacant room. Sue signalled to Ben with an assuring nod that she would be safe and he was to remain with Ralph.

As the door to the vacant room closed with a forceful thud, Glen turned, and with a firm yet friendly tone, asked Sue to sit at the table. He took a second seat adjacent to her, and inhaled slowly before commencing his explanation. Although he out ranked her, she had out manoeuvred him at the moment, and he knew it.

"What I am about to reveal to you, Sue, is beyond confidential. It is secret. If it gets into the wrong hands, we both could end up as expendable corpses on the burgeoning heap of the naïvely unwary, as could your partner and possibly Ralph. Understood?"

"Understood, Sergeant."

Glen had regained the upper hand at that moment, and Sue knew it.

"Please call me Glen. I'm confident that we're going to get to know each other very well over the course of time. I'm still with Commercial Crime and here working undercover on a file with international implications. From what I can gather, Sue, you came across a murder scene which has international drug connections. I don't have any more information on your relationship than that. I do know that you have a reputation for integrity as does your partner. I would appreciate it very much if you could bring me up to speed on what you know."

Sue sat silently starring at Glen, not knowing if he was one of the white-hatted good guys or one of the black hatted bad guys, or any combination of good and bad. She would feel far less vulnerable with Sir Ben by her side. She needed to gain leverage.

"This case involves my partner. So, we need to bring him into the conversation immediately," she ardently announced. Her demeanour let Glen know that there was no wiggle room with her demand if he wanted her cooperation.

Glen paused, realising that the table had been turned once again. Their bantering thus far had been a Backgammon game where skill could be momentarily inverted with the luck of a throw of the dice.

"OK. I'll call him in." He picked up the phone. "Ralph, ask Sue's partner to join us in room number two. You and I will talk later."

"Ben, this is Sergeant Glen Anderson, Commercial Crime Section from Winnipeg," Sue said snappily. She then invited Ben to take a seat. She summarised the situation before concluding in a confident tone, "We can trust him."

With Ben present, the jousting for control quickly gave way to an agreement for respectful collaboration.

Glen began with a reemphasis on the imperative for secrecy. "As I was explaining to Sue, I am an accountant. We set up Coast Accounting as a cover for my investigation into what we initially thought was a commercial crime case involving money laundering. The Bayview Hotel seemed to fit the profile but that turned out not to be the case. Ho is completely clean."

"Does Ralph know that?" Sue inquired. From a strategic perspective, she would be less defensive about any conversations she might have with Ralph on each evening visit if she knew the answer to that question.

"I'll let him know before I leave."

"OK. That will impact how we interact with him."

"The Bayview Hotel may have an indirect connection," Glen continued. "We suspect that one of the traffickers is staying at a local hotel when he wants to meet with clients. He rents cars but we don't know any more."

"I've asked Ralph to keep a record of licence plates and related litter for an anthropology research project I'm conducting," Ben added. "If Ralph is not aware of who you are, I could ask him to make special note of the identity of hotel guests with licence numbers and makes of the vehicles. He knows that I am a junior constable, so wouldn't think twice about my further request."

"Good idea, Ben," Glen confirmed. "Let me continue. By day, I am Glen the accountant. By night, I'm Glenda, the undercover agent supposedly trolling not as a drag queen but dragging the dregs of Lower Main Street for intelligence. I've facetiously earned the reputation of 'goddess of the night' by some of my colleagues."

"Haven't heard that nocturnal accolade before," Ben murmured with a lighthearted huff.

Glen politely accepted his comedic comment with a shrewd smile of his own before continuing. "I suspected that the circumstances surrounding the murder victim were somehow intertwined in the money laundering case. But that's as far as I got before someone slashed her throat. The trail went cold like her body as her blood drained unceremoniously into the ground. Major Crime is convinced that it was a professional hit but don't know who is responsible and have absolutely no leads at this time."

A silence filled the room as Sue and Ben intentionally exchanged glances seeking concurrence to contribute to the crucible of facts. Without revealing sources, they filled in many of the blank spaces, merely alluding to local intelligence sources close to the deceased.

As Glen had emphasised with the overlay of security associated with his intelligence, Sue reiterated her heightened caveat related to corruption within the hierarchy of the Force, government, the judicial system, and commercial businesses, amongst others. Both Sue and Ben confirmed Glen's suspicion regarding a connection to Central America drug cartels. They also validated his wariness that the West Coast had become a new battle space for the competing drug warlords as they plied their violence in efforts to secure potentially productive untapped markets, with Sechelt being a staging area for additional operations.

"We refer to these types of operation in the military as FOBs," Ben interjected. "Forward Operating Bases. They can be clandestine but are almost always lethal in execution."

Glen acknowledged the accuracy of Ben's operational experience. He then meticulously focused on his and Sue's accumulated hard evidence and detailed gems of intelligence, all the while transferring his astonished gaze from one to the other.

"The two of you are damn good. I've been working on this file with a small team of crime analysts for six months. The two of you have been involved for six days, and know more about what is going down than myself, Sub-Division Drug Section and Major Crime combined. OK. So how can I help the diamond duo?"

"As we've mentioned, both Ben and I don't know who we can trust given the depth and breadth of corruption and cover up, and the extent of the lethal consequences if we misjudge. There are international implications for the murder and the drugs. These players are particularly vicious as we witnessed by the level of brutality with this murder. The drugs and the murder are connected. We can't solve one without prying open Pandora's Box and delving into the other. The drugs are sourced from Central America and that means Sub-Division Drug Section needs to become involved in addition to other Federal government departments. Quite frankly, we don't know what our next steps should be. Our default mode must be to trust no one and suspect everyone."

"I completely agree with your assessment, Sue. Corrupt circumstances dictate the need for radical strategies. Hear me out before you jump all over me and accuse me of being completely off my rocker."

Sue and Ben exchanged befuddled expressions at Glen's preannouncement of a potentially far-fetched strategy from a conservative strait-laced charted accountant masquerading as a goddess of the night. He was a mixture of staid yet eccentric, traditional yet idiosyncratic. How off the beaten path could a long-in-the-tooth RCMP Senior NCO accountant stray?

"Are we talking 'Alice in Wonderland down the rabbit hole' strange?" Ben inquired with his familiar baritone chuckle.

Glen's proposal would indeed make the Mad Hatter appear ultra-orthodox.

Chapter 10

Glen highly recommended Corporal Kaplanski as a team confidant. He had worked undercover in Toronto for close to three years on an international drug case that also involved motorcycle gangs. He knew or knew of some of the players from South and Central America. There was certainly no love lost between Kaplanski and the cartel tribes. "He may be an obnoxious harasser but he has a reputation of a tenacious bulldog when it came to enforcement. He is fearless in his fight. When push comes to shove, he is as honest as the day is long."

Sue reeled at the notion of being in the same Division as Kaplanski, let alone on the same detachment, or worse working on the same case. She was aware of Glen's reputation for integrity. But his proposal pushed the limits of what might be tolerable under any circumstances. She gained some solace from the fact that Glen was famous if not infamous for off the record, behind the barn, unique *tête-à-tête* disciplinary encounters with those within his sphere who stepped out of line.

Ben stood sentinel beside his partner. His support for Sue was absolute. He drew his dark eyebrows together and scowled sternly in opposition, all the while levelling his exacting focus on Sergeant Anderson like a sniper's laser aiming beams.

Glen only had to look at Ben to understand where he stood. "I get your message loud and clear, Ben. But think of it this way. If Kaplanski is working for me out of Winnipeg, the probability that he will come in contact with either of you is significantly lower than if he remains here on Detachment."

Ben scratched his chin and grimaced while starring defiantly at the ceiling. "You're right," he acknowledged reluctantly. "He certainly wouldn't be serendipitously dropping into our crime scenes anymore."

"Let me give you a little background info, and you keep this under your Stetsons." Glen made eye contact with both of his potential comrades who accepted this supplementary condition. "The Kaplanski you know isn't the Kaplanski who joined the Force. He went native from being deeply undercover without appropriate support for such a long period of time while associating with unscrupulous traffickers, and bikers who audaciously brandished all the colours of wings, including venerated black. He had been playing the part of a bad guy so long that he had forgotten how to be a good guy. That's not an excuse for his harassment of Sue. Instead, it's just an explanation."

A pause filled the room as Sue and Ben pondered Glen's rationalisation. At its hiatus, the stillness seemed intensely rapt.

"One last point," Glen continued in a more fatherly conciliatory tone. "If either of you end up working undercover with the scum of the earth, you too may find yourself having to deal with Ebenezer Scrooge's ghosts from Christmas past with the unresolved emotions lying in wait that appear as surreal shadows to trip you up when you least expect them and never want them. The Force was remiss in not providing psychological debriefings and transition counselling to him when he came out. They took that into consideration when finding him not guilty of Sue's harassment allegation. I emphasise that his perfidious misconduct is not an excuse. Sometimes, shit happens and you just have to accommodate it."

A moderating silence settled in the room before Ben mumbled inquisitively to Sue, "Wings?"

"I'll explain later," she whispered with a disgusted contortion of her entire face. Ben could only imagine the potential of the interpretation. Whatever it was, he sensed that it hadn't been one of the learning outcomes in any of the courses in his anthropology degree.

Glen continued with his summary of Kaplanski's lurid career. "Kaplanski will be immediately transferring to the Musical Ride in Ottawa where he will be assigned to shovel horseshit by day under the supervision of a female fellow sergeant who has the reputation of intimidating the Staff Sergeant Major on occasion. By night, he will be assigned to re-establish contact with some of his previous associates in the drug world. Within a fortnight, I will be back at my desk in Winnipeg at which time Kaplanski will be standing in front of me with his heels sharply together. He will understand in no uncertain terms why he spent a week unceremoniously shovelling horseshit."

Sue smiled sarcastically. Literally, shovelling shit was a more appropriate disciplinary outcome than counselling or attending a harassment course, had her complaint been founded. Her father was a warrant officer in the military and she could remember those times when he would give young soldiers the option of being formally changed for a foolish offence and appearing before the commanding officer, or taking the sergeant major's informal discipline. Those who were astute chose the latter.

"This is how we will operate," Glen outlined. "You feed all your intel to me. I will coordinate the investigations and direct Kaplanski as appropriate. When the cases are solved, both of you will be given top billing. Let me reiterate. You should never see Kaplanski again and he will only be mentioned in my final report in the small print. Agreed?"

Both Sue and Ben blinked with concurrence and replied in unison. "Agreed."

"I will remain involved because of the known link to money laundering. I can guarantee that. Let me explain why. There are a few senior officers who owe me pickets for favours I did for them over the years. In brief, I covered their stupid asses on more than one occasion when they were foolish constables and junior NCOs motivated by misguided mischief. They owe me big time and I remind them of their indebtedness on a regular basis, and always in a professional polite manner. This modus operandi works well for all concerned. It just seems to solidify their obligation."

There are formal policies and procedures that are taught in Depot basic training and then there is field training, Ben reflected. You can't officially teach Glen's survival skills in a classroom. The path where he and Sue were headed would demand a more flexible strategic perspective, and indisputable honesty and loyalty. They were heading into unknown enemy territory with known and unknown landmines. Ben had rapidly learned that while serving in Afghanistan. Even if you knew where the IEDs were, they could still blow up in your face. This became a stark reality to him when his engineering colleague was killed while disarming the landmine.

Glen summed up the analysis. "If you haven't already connected the dots, let me do so. Your murder is connected to the drugs which is connected to the money laundering which is connected back to the murder, and God knows what else. Solve one and you solve all. Put another way, expose the malicious malignant content of one of Pandora's boxes and you expose the maggots in the other two boxes. If executed incorrectly, the maggots may escape as diseased fleas to become contagious hosts laying their infectious eggs elsewhere."

Glen locked the door behind him. The diamond duo headed for their patrol car as their new partner re-entered the hotel office and returned the key to its empty hook. He met Ralph's inquisitive glance with a questioning frown.

"Regret the secrecy, Ralph. It's a police matter regarding the murder case. Sue said that I can't say more than that for now."

Ralph merely smiled and nodded in a non-judgemental accepting manner in acknowledgement of Glenda's lifestyle.

"Regarding CRA and the Bayview Hotel, I can confirm that the case is closed. So, how can I help you with your paper?"

"I think that I'm OK for now. I just wanted to make sure that I hadn't missed anything for this final case study assignment. You know how fastidious accounting instructors are when it comes to grading assignments. For reasons of confidentiality, I won't mention the Bayview in my analysis."

Ralph watched his mentor as he ambled out of the office and into the misty night not certain if Glen was headed back to his office or whether Glenda was en route to Lower Main Street. Either way, he knew that he did not possess all the circumstantial facts for his term paper. He resigned himself to the status quo. It was better for Glen to be deceptive with him than to say nothing. The first lines of Robert Service's poem, *The Cremation of Sam McGee*, soundlessly reverberated from the depths of his ever-inquisitive mind, 'There are strange things done in the midnight sun by the men who moil for gold.' For now, he was content to be the unassuming humble night auditor.

Chapter 11

"You smell like horseshit, Corporal Kaplanski. Where have you been?"

"I tried out for the Musical Ride but unfortunately didn't make the first cut. In a weakened moment, I thought that I could sit on a horse safe and sound in my red serge and learn to sing 'Rose Marie' like a good little Mountie. Then it dawned on me that I'm allergic to horses and can't carry a tune."

"Well, maybe it just wasn't meant to be. Am I communicating clearly with you, Corporal?"

"Yes, Sergeant."

"Good. Now have a seat, Bill, and call me Glen."

"Yes …" he paused momentarily as he reassessed his environment and the essence of this underlying conversation. "Yes, Glen."

"Wonderful, Bill. I have a proposal that you might find very appealing given your background. I also have a leave pass here which you haven't signed for whatever reason. It looks like you want to spend some time in the Cayman Islands and Mexico. I've heard that the beaches are wonderful and the nightlife entertaining."

Kaplanski tilted his head and with a Cheshire cat grin, replied. "My oversight for not signing the leave request sergeant. Excuse me. I meant to say Glen. I don't deal with rejection well and after failing to be accepted onto the Musical Ride, my childhood dream, I felt that I needed a holiday."

Glen peered over the rim of his coffee cup. "I have been remiss in not consulting with you fully on the case." He spent the balance of the morning briefing Bill on the file. "You did an outstanding job with the bike gangs in Toronto putting a dent in their drug operation. We now need to put a crimp in operations of the money laundering operations. We suspect that some boys and girls from Central America may be importing drugs into Vancouver via the Sunshine Coast and laundering the proceeds. No surprise to you is the fact that biker gangs on the West Coast may be involved also. Any questions thus far?"

"No questions, Glen."

"Because you recently spent time in uniform in E Division, you must stay clear of any connection to British Columbia. You report directly to me. The E Division Drug Section will take care of everything west of the Rockies. I will be taking the lead for Commercial Crime. Primarily on your request but also as I see fit, we will rendezvous in a myriad of other locations to debrief. This file is no cakewalk but it will be far less stressful than your Toronto assignment. I can guarantee that. You will literally have time to relax on the beaches and soak up the rays."

Kaplanski thought for a very brief moment. "I've also heard that the Grand Caymans and Mexico have some of the best beaches. When do I depart on Vacation Airlines?"

The narcotic-like rush of yet another mission was readily evident once again. Also present was the ominous tugging of destiny's gravity causing his tinnitus to ring with increasing intensity as his heart pumped harder and his eyes darted in a chaotic pattern, ever conscious of the menacing malice of invisible shadows. He knew these physiological responses because they always accompanied him during the sleepless nights when he aimlessly patrolled the streets in his own car with his police scanner that kept him connected when connectedness seemed elusive. It was a maddening habit but one over which he seemed not to have complete control. But undercover work provided him with the ambience he needed to quench these seemingly unquenchable thirsts, if even only temporarily.

"Anticipating your positive response, Bill, I took the initiative to put together a vacation package that includes your identification papers, tickets, pesos and other useful currencies, in addition to literature on tourist sites that you might find to your liking. Memorise the contents carefully with particular attention to your contacts. You know the drill on what to pack and what to leave behind. For the next week, you will be brushing up on your Spanish language skills."

"I always did like tacos and enchiladas," he quipped as he stood up to shake his new supervisor's hand.

"And one last point. If you do a good job, your application for the Musical Ride would be favourably reviewed."

"Ah … no thanks. One thing I learned from the last week's experience is that I detest, abhor, loathe and despise horses with a passion, if for no other reason than horseshit stinks."

"Lessons learned are wise teachings, Corporal Kaplanski," Glen confirmed with a reassuring fatherly pat on his shoulder, as he accompanied his newest colleague to the door. "Be safe in the sandbox, Bill. Most of these folks do not have a sense of humour and do not take kindly to others meddling in their affairs."

***

Sue scanned her incoming emails. Out of habit, she didn't open anything from sources she didn't recognise. She had recently granted this new one permission. 'I understand that the weather on the West Coast has improved and the forecast is for continued clear skies. I'd be pleased to assist you with your income tax return this year.'

"All OK?" Ben inquired.

"All OK, partner. All OK."

Chapter 12

Ralph had convinced Ho to install surveillance video cameras on the hotel property, especially the locations furthest away from the flood-lit canopy adjacent to the office. Ho was further motivated when Ralph informed him that the premiums for property insurance would be reduced. Ho eagerly signed the cheque without any hesitation when he added that the purchase would also be a tax deduction.

The new motion detector lighting tended to deter prowlers while corralling those who still sought the seclusion of the shadows in the short-term parking stalls immediately across from the entrance where Ralph could more readily monitor movements on the newly installed CCTV screen in the office. An added benefit was a longer nightly stopover by Sue and Ben who methodically scrutinised the traffic with each visit. At the end of a recent shift, they asked for a copy of the most current surveillance showing an individual and his car. Ralph indicated that he was a less frequent but routine hotel guest who consistently requested the room at the furthest end of the hotel.

"He always pays in U.S. cash and leaves a hefty tip, sometimes a few hundred dollars." The hotel registration records indicated that he gave an address in Mexico City. Sue followed up only to discover that the address proved to be false. His passport number that Ralph noted was valid for Don Miguel Garcia. The licence number on the rental vehicle confirmed that it had been registered to a Don Miguel Garcia with the same false street address in Mexico City that the driver gave to Ralph each time he stayed at the hotel.

"I'll email this intel to Glen," Sue advised Ben.

"OK. I'll send the images from the surveillance to Alejandra just on the off chance that she might recognise them."

"Hold back on the name for now," Sue suggested. "I'm uncertain about the implications of releasing his identity too soon. Prudence may be the better policy at this early stage."

Glen acknowledged receipt of the email almost immediately and indicated that he would get back to Sue.

Before Glen replied, Ben received his response from Alejandra marked URGENT. She recognised the CCTV images and identified him as Don Miguel Garcia, but, to the best of her recollection, he had no fixed address. She believed that he could be from Crozal, Belize or Chetumal on the Yucatan peninsula close to Belize. She had never met him formally but saw him from the shadows in the company of other senior unsavoury individuals in the hierarchy of the cartel. He went by the alias El Negociador la Navaja – the Negotiator the Razor, because he would slit the throats of those who did not comply with the dictates of the cartel. "He lives up to his reputation so be extremely careful particularly if he has been drinking," Alejandra warned.

"I think that we've found the murderer of the tyranny," Ben announced to Sue with a tone that left no doubt as to his heightened sense of imminent threat and need for increased vigilance.

"No question. We send this to Glen straightaway. If it is our man, then Glen needs to pass this intel along to Kaplanski immediately," Sue responded with a sense of urgency.

"And we need to be exceptionally wary when we visit Ralph next," Ben reacted still with an amplification in his voice. "I'm thinking that we don't mention this to Ralph because he may change the way he deals with Don Miguel Garcia, even subconsciously. I do not want to imagine the consequences if the target thinks that we are onto him. One slit throat is one too many for my short career."

Sue paused and nodded in agreement. "I agree for now. But we need direction from Glen. Like you, I do not want to consider the consequences for Ralph, or for us if there is an internal investigation. I don't mind taking statements but do not want to be on the other side of the interview table giving statements, especially to Internal Investigations. A short career may be an understatement. It would not look good on our resumes when applying for future employment."

Glen replied to Sue's email within moments. 'Keep your distance and wait for instructions. In the interim, check with my protégé to ascertain if he can confirm the current location of the vehicle.'

'Subject paid ten days in advance and isn't due to checkout until the end of the week,' Sue emailed back. 'No indication of whereabouts. Apparently, it's not uncommon for him to leave early and never officially checkout. I will inquire with the rental car company and advise.'

'I have the cavalry standing by for immediate deployment once we can confirm location,' Glen updated.

Within the hour, Sue got back to Glen. 'The vehicle has not been returned to the rental company. The rental contract gave local region as the intention of the driver. They checked previous rental agreements that listed mid Vancouver Island and Sunshine Coast as potential destinations. The driver had previously put on in excess of one thousand kilometres over several days for former rentals. The rental company will let me know when the car is returned.'

The chilled hiatus was worrisome for Sue. It was beyond worrisome for Ben who could not fathom the image of Alejandra's slit throat or how he would react.

"He'll turn up. Every detachment has been advised," Sue calmly reassured her partner. "He's more than likely somewhere mid Island between North Cowichan and Campbell River, or on the west side of the Island around Tofino. There aren't that many roads and he can't go unnoticed too long. This is the game of cat and mouse. After we solve this one, routine night shifts will be unbelievably boring. Welcome to the world of policing. Ninety-nine-point-nine percent of the time is mind-numbing dull, and the point one percent is heart-pounding excitement."

"Boring would be graciously accepted right now," Ben uttered. "Do you have any anti-acid meds? I think that Ralph's high-quality coffee and day-old cholesterol have hit an all-time low for my constitution."

"We can stop at a 24-hour drug store for some." After a quiet gap, Sue muttered with reservation in her voice, "I never thought in a million years that I would say this, but I hope that Kaplanski is OK."

"Alejandra is on the top of my worry list. But I'll second your concern for your previous supervisor," Ben muttered back. "He is a harassing asshole but he's still a Member of the Force."

Chapter 13

Sue greeted her partner at the start of the shift the next morning. "The shift supervisor wants to see you, something to do with a dead body. I didn't get the impression that it was ours because he just wanted to see you," Sue advised. "I'll wait for you by the car."

"What's up, Corp? Sue mentioned that you wanted to see me about a dead body," Ben inquired inquisitively. Since being assigned to Sue as his trainer, he had never done anything alone. He felt a little uncomfortable now standing in front of their supervisor without her beside him.

"A female body was found in Sechelt. Apparently, your personal phone number was the last number she tried to call on her cell phone. A helicopter will be here momentarily to fly you over, so get Sue to drive you to the landing zone. Sechelt GIS want you to ID the body, if you can, and ask you why she called you. That's all I know. Please keep me informed, as I need to update the Detachment Commander. So, what have you been up to?"

"Don't know, Corp. Only been to the Sunshine Coast once. But I'll keep you in the loop."

"You look like death warmed over, Ben," Sue commented on his gaunt ashen complexion and sunken stature.

"Let's mount up. We need to talk," Ben mumbled out of earshot of others mingling in the parking lot. Once in their patrol car, he reiterated the essence of the conversation with the shift NCO. "I emailed Alejandra but she hasn't got back to me."

"OK. I'll drive you to the LZ. I'll text Glen and ask for direction. We don't know that it is Alejandra for sure."

Ben rapidly rattled off a number of questions and scenarios. "Who else would it be? She's the only person in Sechelt who has my cell number. So, if not her, who else would it be? If I have to ID her corpse, I'm not sure how I'll respond. Let me know what Glen says ASAP." He then paused for a moment. "Where you are my trainer, can you request to accompany me?"

Sue re-entered the detachment and returned to Ben within a minute.

"I'm not thinking that your request was received favourably," Ben blurted out before Sue could shut the car door.

"The corporal said that he was short-staffed and I couldn't be spared to accompany you. He figures that you should be back before the shift ends. Remember that I'm only a phone call or text away. And we don't know one hundred percent that it is Alejandra." Her thoughts were running parallel to Ben's. Who else could it be? She needed to plan a course of action to support him. In the interim, she needed to remain calm and positive.

"OK, Sue. But let me know what Glen says as soon as you hear back from him. Mark your email URGENT. I'd like to know his response ideally before or as soon as possible after I land in Sechelt."

"You'll be OK, Ben," Sue assured her partner. "I have the greatest of confidence in you. Think of it this way. You'll have more experience in your first six months of field service than the vast majority of Members have in their entire career."

"Bring on the boring night shifts," Ben muttered with his customary disquieted huff.

"I'll second you on that, Partner." Privately, Sue assessed that this game of cat and mouse was being played with ever changing rules and roles. Mice were adopting non-traditional feral feline roles, while cats were on the souris unfamiliar defensive.

***

"We're approaching Sechelt," the pilot announced. "You alright, Ben? You're looking a bit green under the gills."

"I'm OK but will be better once we land. I don't do well in small aircraft. Give me a 777 any day." In reality, his stomach was in knots just thinking about Alejandra lying naked exposed and abandoned on an impersonal cold marble slab in a morgue. Equally unappealing was the prospect of being questioned by GIS. He racked his brain trying to figure out how the deceased would have had his phone number, if the cadaver wasn't Alejandra.

"Constable McLeod, I'm Constable Stuart. My instructions are to drive you to the hospital and take you down to the morgue."

"Call me Ben. Can we sit for a moment until I get my land legs under me? Helicopters are not my favourite mode of transportation." He quickly texted Alejandra again.

"OK. Did they tell you anything about the body?" Constable Stuart asked.

"Only that it's female."

"You want to prepare yourself. I understand that whoever killed her did a real number on her. She suffered multiple stab wounds to the face and neck. There are some real sick psychopaths out there."

Ben didn't reply. Instead, he tried to prepare himself for the worst-case scenario. One horrific murder scene was enough. Images of his flashlight beam on the bloodied tranny in the alley grasped his throat to the point that he was starting to experience trouble swallowing and breathing. The image of a second gruesome corpse might send him into cardiac arrest, even if, by a slight chance, it wasn't Alejandra. He only hoped that the blood would be washed off the cadaver. Flashbacks from Afghanistan of blown up bodies and dismembered limbs raced in his mind.

At the hospital, Constable Stuart led him to the morgue. He checked his cell phone for messages from Sue or Alejandra. The screen was blank which left him more alone than he could ever have imagined. He was on his own.

"Ben, this is Corporal Davidson from our GIS Section."

"I understand that you've been briefed on the case Constable McLeod," Davidson spoke gruffly and in a manner void of any emotion. "We need you to identify the body, if possible. It's pretty badly slashed up. Then we'll need to ask you how your cell number got on her phone. It was the last number she attempted to call."

Ben followed him into the morgue. The body was laid supine on the cold bleached white marble slab, covered with an equally featureless white plastic sheet. Ben took a deep breath. The lab technician pulled back the cover. The sight of the corpse strangled his breath. His words wouldn't come.

"Who is she?" Corporal Davidson demanded in an accusatory tone.

After what seemed to be an eternal pause, Ben whispered almost inaudibly, "I don't know who she is. I've never seen her before."

"Are you certain?"

"I'm positive. She looks older than my grandmother," Ben retorted assuredly. He could feel the anxiety immediately draining from every pore in his body. The pace of the relief was accelerating. He experienced unsettling vertigo for a few moments as his physiology was altered with the jubilant realisation that the corpse was not Alejandra. How could he be experiencing a narcotic-like rush in the presence of horrific violence and euphoric relief?

His inquisitor's voice became friendlier. "Damn. We were hoping that you would be able to shed some light on the case. We actually thought that the murder on the Island that you were recently involved in might be related to this somehow."

"Major Crime from Sub-division is handling the Island murder. I'm just a junior constable still on probation and under supervision of my trainer. Very sorry, but can't help."

"So, I'm left scratching my head. I don't understand how your phone number ended up on her cell phone?"

"I have no idea," Ben blurted in an equally perplexed expression. "It's as much a mystery to me also."

"I'm not accusing you of anything, Constable McLeod. Just covering all bases. The thought had crossed my mind that she might have been related to you, perhaps your grandmother. She's too old to be your girlfriend unless you're into cougar grannies," Davidson jested sarcastically. Black humour could be useful amongst cops who walked amongst the dead.

"Maybe she punched in my number by mistake," Ben reacted more out of exhilarated relief than keen investigated supposition. "I have set my phone to block all incoming calls that I haven't given permission to. I then delete all junk without scrutinising further. It's my standard security protocol."

"Maybe." Corporal Davidson paused and then replied with an inquisitive gesture. "Interesting possibility. Hold on a second." He leafed through the file stopping on one entry. "Are you sure that you're just a junior constable? Did you do any investigative police work before you joined the Force?"

"Just an undergraduate degree at UVic. Why do you ask?"

"How would you like to join GIS?"

"Ah … why do you ask?" Ben queried with a slight chuckle. This was the first time since his day started that he felt any sense of relief let alone joviality.

"Looking at her phone records, the deceased called another number a few times. It's very close to your number, just out by two digits. I bet that that's it. Let me make a call before we head back to my office."

The ambiance had changed from abrupt and accusatory to collegial and beholden. By the time they had arrived at the office, Corporal Davidson was gleeful with the revelation. The other telephone number was registered to the daughter of the deceased who provided an address for her mother. The daughter explained that her mother never used speed dial, but instead dialled by hand. So she was prone to making fat finger errors.

"At the residence, a deceased male body has been located. Looks like we may have a murder suicide," Davidson advised Ben. "Sure you don't want a transfer to our GIS Section?"

"No thanks but concede the gracious offer. I've had my fill of gruesome crime scenes for a while."

"I very much appreciate your assistance, Ben," Corporal Davidson concluded as he shook Ben's hand with genuine gratefulness. "I'll be calling your supervisor shortly and passing along accolades. Constable Stuart will drive you to Gibsons Landing where you'll be meeting a floatplane that will take you back home to the Big Island. Again, thanks for all your assistance."

"The gratitude is all mine," Ben replied with his warming smile, all along relieved that the cadaver wasn't Alejandra. He checked his phone for messages from Sue or Alejandra. Nothing. But this time he was less stressed. His text to Sue briefly read, 'All OK, Partner. All OK. On my way home.'

"I haven't eaten all morning. I understand that there is a very good café close by. Can we stop there for a bite? I'd prefer not to fly on an empty stomach," Ben prompted Constable Stuart.

"Absolutely. Know the café well. Most of the patrols stop in for muffins or cookies. They have a new cook who bakes the best pastries on the Sunshine Coast," she boasted smugly. "I could do with a little sugar uptake myself."

Constable Stuart parked in the courtyard adjacent to the café. The window to the kitchen was open and greeted passers-by with aromas that caused their mouths to salivate like Pavlov's drooling dog. Alejandra stood by the counter.

"Love the fragrance of fresh baked goods," Ben uttered loudly in order to attract the baker's attention.

As they entered, Alejandra was already inconspicuously approaching from the kitchen. Ben starred at her with a myriad of emotions painted on his face from elation to quizzical, to annoyed, to exhausted, to accelerated, to relieved and finally to complete endearment. He exclaimed, "I had one of your muffins a while back. I'd like to order a few to go. And can I get your recipe? Perhaps you would send it to me if I gave you my email address. Here, let me write it down on this napkin. I apologise. The other time I was here, I had given you my email but I must have written it down incorrectly because I haven't received a reply and I recall that you said you would."

Alejandra returned to the kitchen where she wrote on the napkin. Ben had paid for his muffins by the time she returned.

"Here is the recipe you asked for. Not replying to your initial request would have been my error. I lost my cell phone recently and have just replaced it with a new telephone number."

Ben took the folded napkin and lovingly slid it into his left breast pocket, pausing momentarily with his hand over his heart in a signalled gesture for Alejandra's benefit. He tracked her eyes as they lowered to his chest. He then extended his hand in gratitude, doubling his hold on top of hers with his other hand. "I cannot thank you enough," he responded all the while gazing into her eyes with a yearning that she could not misinterpret. Just touching her hand and feeling her pulse caused the frisson of love to flood to the forefront of his feeling. He could not stave off his emotions. Instead, he could only mask them with the adroitness of his professionalism. With what he had been through on the emotional rollercoaster ride leading up to this intended assignation, it was all he could do at this juncture not to take her in his arms with the intention of never letting her go. But that would have to wait for the enticing tryst that Alejandra had previously suggested at the finale of their previous rendezvous on the beach.

Ben texted Alejandra while waiting for the floatplane at Gibsons. 'We need to talk sooner rather than later. I can't die of a heart attack at my young age. Technology is great but need one-on-one face time.'

Her reply came immediately. 'Agreed. Name the time and place. TOY'

'TOY?' Ben texted back.

'Thinking of you'.

'TOY' appeared on Alejandra's screen.

Chapter 14

"Constables Archer and McLeod, in my office, please."

Ben and Sue exchanged restrained quizzical glances and shrugged their shoulders in unison like synchronised swimmers.

"What's up now?" Ben whispered, all the while surmising that it couldn't be all that bad or it was mildly horrific if they were both being summoned by the shift supervisor.

"Don't know," Sue murmured back as she raised her eyebrows and widened her expression.

"Yes, Corp," she acknowledged out loud.

"Received a note from Sechelt GIS. I understand that you helped solve their murder case, Ben, despite the fact that you couldn't ID the deceased. Well done!"

Ben nodded with a gestured smile. "Always pleased to be of service. It was a learning experience." In all the exhilaration of the roller coaster ride and then seeing Alejandra again, he had forgotten that Davidson had promised to send over an accolade.

"And Sue. Our Ident folks said that you did a superior job securing the scene on our murder case. They recommended that you instruct all new field officers."

"Thanks Corp," Sue acknowledged.

"The Detachment Commander has directed that I place a commendation entry on both of your personnel files. Don't let it go to your heads."

Both of his patrol officers smiled in response.

"Now get out of my office. And keep the community safe tonight. No more dead bodies, please!"

"Yes, Corp," both responded in harmony.

As they walked to the parking lot, Sue purposely bumped into her partner and uttered with a reassuring buoyant smile, "Bravo Zulu, partner. I looked that up on the web. If I'm not mistaken, I think that it means 'well done' in military jargon."

Ben bowed in gratitude of her initiative to learn a little more about his military service. "Ack, partner, and same to you. Ack is a short-term for acknowledged."

"And did you get to see Alejandra?"

Ben's beaming palpable expression said it all.

"Glen got back to me. Glenda is back in town and wants to meet us on Lower Main Street around one. His message was terse. I'll text Ralph and let him know that we'll be late for our predictable ten after the hour caffeine and cholesterol break."

"OK. But don't forget that we are seeking the ninety-nine point nine eight per cent mind-numbing boring shift where we simply cut and paste the previous night patrol report," Ben quipped with his signature baritone chuckle.

"Sir Ben has returned," Sue mused. She was looking forward to receiving an update from the goddess of the night.

***

"Hello Glenda. Haven't seen you around for a while."

"Constable Archer, it's good to see you too. Is this your new partner?"

"I'm Constable McLeod, Glenda."

Once outside the audible orbit of other worshippers of Nyx who populate the shadows and creviced conclaves of the urban landscape, Glen brought Sue and Ben up to date.

"Kaplanski is on the ground in Cancun. He spent some time in Toronto reacquainting himself with a few of his old biker buddies. To set up his story, he explained to them that he had been in the Grand Caymans and Mexico establishing new business relationships for an import export enterprise, and was on his way back. From Toronto, he flew to Myrtle Beach, North Carolina where he got picked up for being drunk and disorderly, and starting a fight in a bar. He spent the night in the local County Mountie drunk tank. He then flew to Dallas where the DEA picked him up for possession of marijuana on a drug sweep. He skipped bail and snuck across the border to Mexico. There is now a warrant out for his arrest. The whole idea was to establish an audit trail for his new assignment."

"If that's what it takes to work undercover, then I've got a little more respect for him," exclaimed Ben. "I'm not sure that I could live that lifestyle."

"That's what it takes and often more," Glen confirmed. "And the game of cat and mouse has only begun."

"It doesn't excuse his harassing," Sue bluntly muttered. "But I have a better appreciation of who he is and what contributed to his unprofessional behaviour."

"On the local front," Glen added, "An informant has confirmed that Don Miguel Garcia has made contact with a local biker gang in an effort to secure their loyalty to the Yucatan cartel. The cartel out of Guatemala got to the bikers first which really annoyed Don Miguel. Apparently, he got into a pushing match and threatened some of the bikers. As a result, he was physically thrown out of their compound and told never to show his face again. What's bothersome is his disappearance. Also of concern is the identity of the Guatemalan agent. We know that the bikers are laundering money and trafficking in the proceeds of their other nefarious crimes. Suffice to say that the cartels have upped the ante on our turf in their drug war. We have every reason to believe that the recent murder of the tranny that you found is just the start."

"Is Kaplanski aware of what's going down here?" Sue asked.

"Yes, and thanks for your intel. I advised his backup in Cancun who said that he is fully aware. Kaplanski did confirm from other new potential business associates that Don Miguel is a psychopath who can't distinguish between right and wrong, and is completely void of emotions. He really goes berserk when he drinks. He lives up to his label, the razor, and will slit your throat for no other reason than you glanced at him. Kaplanski is happy that Don Miguel is here with us and not in Yucatan with him. Otherwise, he is very much enjoying his vacation time playing the part of the wheeler and dealer and soaking up the rays on the beaches."

"I don't know who I would prefer least, Don Miguel and the cartels in Central America or al Qaeda and the Taliban in Afghanistan," Ben huffed while methodically shaking his head slowly from side to side.

"Be really careful in the sandbox folks," Glen summed up with sincere concern. "Neither of you have experience in this coliseum populated with gladiators of this ruthless calibre. So, just to let you know, it will heat up exponentially before it cools down, and that downside may take a very long time."

"How long is long?" Ben asked hesitantly. He had Alejandra to think about as if her safety ever left his mind.

"Months, often years, occasionally decades. Some of these players never forget, and never is a very long time.

"That long," Ben muttered. Alejandra had best remain Marcelle Santos.

***

"Ralph, you there, hiding in the back?"

"I'm here, Sue. The beans are brewed. I picked up two fresh donuts in addition to the day-olds, which seemed to be exhibiting wrinkles consistent with an extra day or two older. For your info, Glen is back in town. He didn't say where he had been. But that's normal."

"Thanks. We'll keep an eye open for Glenda," Sue confirmed. "We don't want any more murders. By the way, have you seen your truant guest around?"

"I've been monitoring the CCTV screen routinely but haven't seen him for a couple of days now."

"How about the regulars who cruise the short-term parking?" Ben followed up nonchalantly so as not to inadvertently heighten Ralph's attention.

"Haven't seen the dark blue Crown Victoria for quite a long time. I'm thinking that the motion lights and video cameras may have frightened him away."

Ben caught his observational innuendo.

"The white Toyota is still a regular client though. But lately it has been doing a double shift. Once around midnight and again around three. I've bookmarked the occurrences on the CCTV so you can review." Ralph scratched his scalp and rubbed his nose all the while pushing his lips from side to side.

"Ah, what's up doc?" Ben queried in his best Bugs Bunny intonation.

"There's something not quite right about his movements. He slowly cruises in on his first trip and tends to park in the same spot. He stays for about the same time before departing with his passenger. Nothing unusual there. But on the second visit, he drives in quickly and parks in the short-term stall farthest away. On his second trip, I haven't seen a passenger and when I checked the CCTV, he seems to be alone. Perhaps the passenger has purposely slunk down in the seat to avoid being tracked by the surveillance camera."

His two coffee guests reviewed the recordings. "You're right," Sue remarked. "It does seem a bit mysterious. Thoughts, partner?"

Ben paused then added, "Certainly different behaviours between the earlier and later visits. Not sure otherwise." He lingered on his thoughts again. "I have a suggestion. Could we leave Ralph one of our traffic cones to be positioned in the entrance lane under the canopy? This way any driver would have to slow to manoeuvre around. The surveillance camera could get a clearer image."

"I like your thinking," Sue affirmed. "Is it doable, Ralph?"

"Absolutely. If nothing else, it will break up the boredom."

Sue and Ben grinned as their amused gazes met. "Boredom is good," they commented with impeccable accord.

Chapter 15

'He's been spotted in Sechelt. Cavalry has been deployed. Am en route also.' Glen's urgent text to Sue announced.

'Thanks. Will advise partner.'

Ben immediately notified Alejandra, suggesting that she leave Sechelt. She reassured him that she would be safe because Don Miguel had never met her.

By the time Ben was on his partner's doorstep, Glen had updated Sue. The situation had escalated. Don Miguel was dead. Patrol officers had been dispatched to a bar where he had started a fight with other patrons. Upon seeing the police, he pulled out a pistol from under his jacket and shot one of the officers. The second officer returned fire. The ambulance had arrived and first responders pronounced Don Miguel dead at the scene. The wounded officer has been transported to hospital in serious but stable condition.

Sue grabbed her cell phone as it boogied across her kitchen table with the vibration of an incoming message. 'Same time and place tonight,' signed Glenda. She showed the text to Ben who reacted cautiously.

"Give me a moment. I'll let Alejandra know."

"I suspect that the shift supervisor will update everyone this evening. So, act surprised," Sue instructed.

***

"Glenda. How are you?"

"I am well, Constable Archer. Terrible to hear the news about the Mountie being shot in Sechelt, but pleased that he is expected to make a full recovery. What's this world coming to?"

"Yes, the news is distressing. Would you like to talk about it, Glenda? Have a seat in the patrol car."

"How are the two of you doing?" Glen inquired.

"Relieved that Don Miguel is tits up, 10-7, out of service. Excuse my language but it fits the deceased. I'm thinking that we haven't heard or seen the last of his or the competing cartels. Drug wars don't subside with just one death. To the contrary, they tend to go exponential."

"An accurate assessment, Sue. Let me bring you up to speed. First things first. Constable Stuart has been air transported to Vancouver General Hospital, but is expected to make a full recovery."

"Oh my God," Ben exclaimed. "Stuart met me when I arrived in Sechelt and drove me to Gibsons."

"Shit happens, Ben, and we need to recover. It's a lesson. We always want to count our blessings every day in this job."

"Got that message loud and clear."

"Before you ask, Sue, I have advised Kaplanski. News travels fast. Kaplanski said that the cartel is suspicious. But they're always suspicious. It comes with their business. Where the cartel found out so fast, I sense that Don Miguel had a tail, and this person immediately informed his employer. Until we can confirm otherwise, we need to believe that there is at least one other set of eyes on us. You know the drill, caution, caution, caution."

"Do we know any more about the identity of those from the Guatemala cartel?" Sue followed up.

"Nothing. But we have every reason to believe that they are in our backyard also. I'm hearing that locally at the street level. Sue, you may want to check in with your informant."

"Will do. I should be seeing her later tonight."

"In addition to the gun, Don Miguel was carrying a razor. Forensics is checking it now for any traces of blood. If we're lucky, we'll be able to establish a link to your murder victim."

"If that connection is made, our Detachment Commander will be ecstatic because he'll be able to clear this murder off his books in record time," Sue commented. "A bonus to all the carnage."

"And when I submit my report, he'll learn that the two of you were instrumental in solving this murder and the related drug trafficking activities. Kaplanski will get an honourable mention, perhaps even a nomination for best supporting role in the Hollywood North Academy Awards."

"Much appreciated, Glen," Sue acknowledged.

"Another funny to pass along," Glen added. "Initial inquiries by Sechelt GIS suggests that a few bikers enticed Don Miguel into the bar where they bought several rounds of tequila and egged him on to start the fight. They weren't flying their colours but were known to the proprietor. They were overheard telling Don Miguel that he should shoot any cop that comes through the door."

"What happened to the bikers?" Ben interrupted. "If they did entice Don Miguel to shoot a cop, then that's conspiracy to commit a criminal offence. Isn't it?"

"You're correct. Immediately after the shooting, the bikers headed out the door and sped away in a car before the police arrived. GIS suspects that they are hiding out until things cool down. Apparently, their motivation stemmed from Don Miguel's physical altercation in their compound. A few of them followed him to Sechelt where they set him up. He was an easy and willing participant. It's a common error in judgement by many badass actors who have this pseudo sense of their inflated bravado and invincibility. They think that they are the biggest meanest SOBs in the arena."

"Then they find out that there is an even bigger badder SOB out there," Sue added. "Don Miguel found out the hard way."

"Last point. I'll be Glenda, the elusive goddess of the night, for the next week or so working on the money laundering file. I'll keep you up to date. Don't forget that we are confident that both cartels have people here. So be very careful in the sandbox. One cop shot is one too many."

Glen exited the car and became Glenda again. Ben texted Alejandra that, despite Don Miguel's demise, other cartel agents were more than likely in Sechelt and perhaps other locations on the Sunshine Coast. She should reconsider relocating. If not, then she was to be extra vigilant and let him know if she recognised anyone or was remotely suspicious of any strangers.

"Coffee and a donut chez Ralph, partner?"

His grin said it all.

Chapter 16

"May I have your attention?" The shift supervisor opened the briefing. "Before the rumour mill grinds too fast, I'd like to bring you up-to-date on the shooting across the water in Sechelt. Constable Stuart is recovering well and is expected to be discharged from hospital by the end of the week. The deceased is, was a member of a criminal element out of Mexico. His death has been reported to the media as part of a money laundering case related to local biker gangs. Our sleepy hollow may be awakened by related external factors, so keep your ears to the ground and report any suspicious activities. Those with informants, push for details. The murder of the female in the alley on our patch may be related. You will see a stronger presence of our GIS and Major Crime out of Sub-Division over the next several days. Be safe out there, folks."

"Have text messages from Glenda and my informant," Sue reported to Ben. "We should also complete extra patrols of the Bayview and chat with Ralph about any suspicious activities. Let's first head out to Lower Main Street. You chat with a few of the other clients when I see my informant. We may meet up with Glenda, if we are lucky."

"10-4, partner. I want to follow-up on the white Toyota, also. It just seems weird that the driver changed his routine at about the same time as we stumbled on the body of the tranny in the alley. It may be nothing but as Sherlock Holmes would suggest to Watson, 'nothing is always an option because no is a decision, perhaps for the status quo'."

***

"Glenda, how are you this evening?" Ben prompted.

"I am well Constable McLeod. Have you found the person who killed the lady in the alley? I'm still terribly upset as are many of my friends."

"Would you like to sit in the car and talk about it?"

"Yes, please."

Sue could not help but hear the introductory conversation and promptly returned to the patrol car.

"I checked with my informant, Glen. She was sternly asked more like pressured to be a devoted distributor for a cartel. But she got the impression that she had no option. Either sign on their dotted line, pledging her unwavering allegiance to their loyalty points plan or go the way of her slain friend. She just knows that there are drugs involved in addition to prostitution. She would hand over all revenues received from merchandise sold and services rendered. She would receive her pittance, ideally without abuse from a malicious backhand or an equally demeaning groping."

"Thanks for that update," Glen complimented. "We haven't hit the 24-carat vein in the goldmine yet but I'm hearing from other sources that we are close. Your murder and the drug cartel activities are all related to the money laundering."

"Any word from Kaplanski?" Sue inquired.

"Yes. He reported that the cartel is suspicious and sending up another enforcer. They seem distrustful of the media reports that Don Miguel was involved in money laundering. If he was, then they think that he was scamming from them. If he wasn't, then why wasn't it reported as drug related? Kaplanski suspects that the cartel is wary of everyone including him, so he will back off for a while."

"Is that a normal procedure, to disengage?" Ben prompted.

"It can be. In the world of undercover work, there are procedures and then there is intuition. You need to always rely on your grassroots intuition and your inherent intelligence when you play this game. In my experience, intuition is the motivation and intelligence informs the decisions."

"OK. What can Ben and I do to help?"

"Keep doing what you've been doing. To date, your intel has been more helpful than anything the supposed experienced investigators have uncovered."

"When last we spoke, there was some indication of a drug war being fought on our turf. Any update?" Sue prompted.

"Kaplanski also reported that the Yucatan and Guatemala cartels are engaged in a turf war over who will control Belize which has become a bloody battle ground. That is part of their reasoning to send up agents to take control of the Sunshine coast. Yucatan and Guatemalan cartel agents are poised to bring the fight to the Pacific Northwest. Our cavalry are ready to engage but we don't know where to deploy because we don't know who these people are. Any intel that you can gather on this would be vital. As always, be safe in the sandbox, *mes amies*."

"Next stop, caffeine and cholesterol, chez Ralph," Ben suggested.

"Ralph, you there?" Sue announced their arrival.

"As always. Got a couple of fresh donuts for my two best customers. Also got the latest scoop from Joan at King's Bakery who heard it from a few of her patrons. Word has it that a few new faces have been putting the squeeze on them and their friends to become entrepreneurs in the community. It's a type of a marketing and sales enterprise with no retirement plan but considerable risk to life and limb if one strays from the defined policies and procedures. There would be grave consequences for non-compliance. In brief, people are not feeling safe."

Sue confirmed his news. "We're hearing the same thing and it's disturbing to say the least."

"Perhaps sacrifices of donuts to Nyx, the goddess of the night, might be in order," Ralph suggested in a jovial tone.

"Got anything new on the white Toyota or other recent short-term clientele in the parking lot or guests in rooms?" Ben asked.

"The traffic cone in the entranceway has slowed the incoming traffic as you suggested. You can review the tapes yourself but I haven't been able to pick out any passenger in the interior of the Toyota on the 3 a.m. visit. All other traffic is normal. Have had a few new guests, mostly couples. Again, nothing out of the norm. I do have reservations for two in two separate rooms for tomorrow night. They will be staying for a week or so. Just have names and credit card numbers to confirm the reservations. I've taken a deposit so the credit cards are legitimate. Both are business-related cards. So, won't know the names until they check in."

"Can you text me as soon as you have the names and licence plate numbers?" Sue asked in a voice that was more of a directive than a request.

"Sure. Can do. I'm sensing that there is a tincture of caution in the need for prompt and precise identification. Is it related to the heightened feeling for caution in Joan's transmission of information from her nocturnal regulars?"

"Could be. Just want to stay on top of what's going on in the community."

Ben nodded quietly all the while maintaining a well-defined reassuring gaze at Ralph in support of his partner's suggestion for an amplified sense for wariness.

"We'll be on a few days off starting tomorrow, Ralph. So please text me with this information as soon as you get it. Also, let us know of anything that seems out of the ordinary, in any way."

"OK. And you take care, also."

Ben added, "I'll be in Sechelt checking out the beaches and cafés. Can you cc me? Sue will forward all messages but it would be easier if I could be in the initial loop."

"Will do, also," Ralph nodded.

Chapter 17

Ben and Alejandra met for dinner at the Wharf Pub overlooking the pebbled beach and bordered by the promenade walkway and the jetty, which Ben assessed as having seen better days, although still functional. It would be a convenient venue for an after-dinner stroll and secluded conversation.

Out of guarded routine, Alejandra scanned the profiles, the mannerisms, and the interactions of the other patrons and employees. A distinct cacophony of voices riveted her attention on two men whose backs were partially turned toward her and Ben. One emitted a daunting laugh accentuated with disdainful bravado. Distress shrouded her eyes as a frightful shiver ran the length of her stiffened spine. She immediately snuggled her face into Ben's embrace to cover her identity.

"Hold me close, Ben, and cover my face, I recognise one of these guys. In fact, I recognise both of them. One is from the Cancun cartel and the other might be from Belize or Guatemala. Isn't this an interesting tempest in the teapot?"

"Elaborate," Ben prompted quizzically.

"Back home, they're arch enemies but here they appear to be the best of friends. I wonder?"

"Blackmail can run upstream," Ben responded with a reed-thin whisper. "Keep close."

"I've never wanted to keep closer to you than right now," she purred, "But not under these guarded circumstances." She lamented that he never knew how many times she had pined for him in her dreams, to be in his arms, to be this close and closer.

"Do you want to leave?"

"No. Like Don Miguel, I don't think that they could identify me because I only saw them from the shadows. We never formally met. The one on the left is an enforcer with the Cancun cartel. I had a relationship with one of his friends who may have bragged to him about that assignation, but perhaps not. I'm not sure. So need to lean on the side of caution."

"OK. Let's slide around to the other side of the booth where you will be out of their direct line of sight. We can just observe for the time being."

"Can I take your order?" the server asked.

"Two glasses of Pinot Noire," Ben answered with a momentary averting of his eyes away from his focused surveillance of the two men. "We may have something to eat later."

Before they needed to refill their goblets, the suspects unexpectedly stood up and hurriedly left the pub. They briskly walked down the wharf where they hopped aboard a tugboat that had stealthily appeared out of the emerging mist and pulled alongside.

"Take my car keys and drive home. I'm going to follow them. I'll text you." With a quick embrace and a hurried kiss, he whispered, "I do worry about you so let me know that you are home and safe."

Ben swiftly traced the steps of the two Central American compatriots. He jumped aboard the tugboat and inquired with the only apparent crewmember, whom he assumed was the captain. "Can I get a ride also?"

"Yeah," the tugboat captain muttered, "as long as you're going to the same place. I'm not too sure where that is except somewhere on the east coast of Vancouver Island, north of Nanaimo. They'll let me know once we are underway. They just pay me really well each time."

"I'm cool with that," Ben agreed. He picked up on the captain's reference to each time. This was not an infrequent occurrence, he surmised.

"Do you know how to cast off?" the captain asked more in a directing tone than a polite inquiry into Ben's mariner skills.

"Sure."

"Then cast off."

After untying the tether, Ben jumped back on board and secured the line. Looking at the captain, he asked, "How much for the ride?"

"That depends."

"Depends of what?" Ben nonchalantly shrugged.

"Why you want to hitch a ride?"

Ben paused to assess the captain's character before selecting a plausible response. He had peaceful contented eyes framed by a placid tolerant expression, yet his mannerism spoke of prudence and wariness of strangers. There was nothing petty about his facial features. He was his own man and certainly nobody's fool.

"I deserted from the US Army out of Fort Lewis because my Unit was being deployed to Afghanistan and I don't believe in the violence of war. I joined the Engineers to build things like bridges and schools and help people, not to destroy structures and traumatise innocent victims caught in the maelstrom of conflicts initiated beyond their peaceful communities."

The tugboat captain's circumspect demeanour morphed into one of understanding and acceptance with Ben's explanation. His chapped seadog lips mutated into a faint smile. With a gentle heartening nod he whispered. "Your ticket is free. I deserted from the US Army during the Vietnam War. I know the feeling and admire your motivation. It was a tough decision for me, leaving everything I knew and loved behind. I think that I know what you're going through. Welcome aboard."

Ben felt a composed sense of safety. The tugboat was not the infamous Jolly Roger and the captain was not the cantankerous and cunning Captain Hook. He hesitantly extended his hand in gratitude. "Much appreciated, captain."

Like his weathered face, the skipper's hand was leathery from the salt sea northern winds that blew down the inside passage. He continued to observe his features carefully for a moment.

Ben had passed his first extant baptism under fire, and it felt good. But quickly he needed to come up with a nom de guerre for his adopted role as a provisional soldier of fortune in the drug war should he be challenged, even if the two suspects failed to reciprocate. Mission success would come with discipline and flexibility but for now he would bring calm to the anxious flurry in his stomach. He needed to retain an emergency supply on antacids in his pockets.

"Call me Relic," the captain mumbled. "I took the name from the TV program, the Beachcombers, which was popular when I arrived on the Sunshine coast back in the day."

"Thanks, Relic." This style of having to think fast on his feet was appealing. Perhaps he'd talk with Glen more about how he could get into this line of police work. But first, he needed to text Alejandra to let her know that he was OK and to confirm that she had arrived home safely. He then needed to text Sue and Glen to explain what he was doing on his days off. Hopefully, he'd be back in time for his next scheduled night shift with his partner.

"Who the hell is he?" the Cancun cartel passenger angrily demanded of the captain in a working-class Spanish vernacular.

"He's with me. One of my mates," Relic replied gruffly as he wrapped his arm around Ben's shoulder.

The objector just stared with a snarly glare at both the captain and his deckhand as he passed Relic an envelope swollen with U.S. currency and instructions. Neither of the fares added anything further to the abrupt rebuffed verbal exchange, but instead reluctantly settled in for the short voyage.

"Can you get me a cup of coffee," Relic asked in a buoyant tone and in an effort to ease the stagnated tension.

"Aye aye, captain," Ben promptly answered as if routine. His intuition and intellect were operating in tandem like smoothly lubricated components. His seafarer response brought an affable wink from Relic.

Ben followed the two suspects into the galley where they poured themselves a coffee and squeezed in around the grimy arborite table that was adorned with all manner of moulded flotsam, reminiscent of what might have been morsels of meals, but was now slim pickings for ship's rats and maritime cockroaches. They then gave Ben a dismissive glare, which brought a temporary sense of reassurance to his guarded optimism. He wouldn't have to declare his pseudonym before he was ready. If prompted, he would need to choose his response wisely but warily. For now, he had a task to complete as the first mate that would extricate him from the antagonism of the galley and into the friendliness of the wheelhouse.

After delivering Relic his coffee, Ben returned to the galley where he poured himself a java from the dregs of the pot that hadn't seen a bristled scouring pad since the day it had been brought aboard, more than likely back in the day as the skipper inferred. The aroma from the captain's stewing java beans and sight of the opaque carafe made Ralph's coffee service and auditor-in-training ambiance resemble the five-star dining room in the Ritz Hotel on Place Vendôme in Paris.

Ben settled into the captain's chair as if routine and leafed through an old Playboy magazine from decades past, replete with soiled finger smudges on the foldout page. The imperceptible murmurs of the mysterious passengers morphed into audible evidence of a conspiracy to import narcotics into the Sunshine Coast and instigate a drug war on the same turf. All those years of learning Spanish in high school and as a second major for his undergraduate degree were now paying dividends. Private tutored lessons from Alejandra had bolstered his vocabulary.

It became readily apparent that the suspect that Alejandra had identified was in fact from the Cancun cartel and the other was from Guatemala. Ben deduced that they had known each other as kids in the Barrio, related somehow, perhaps cousins. They had subsequently migrated to their respective competing cartels out of coincidence but kept in close contact. They were now colluding for collective benefits, having confirmed a furtive alliance. They had known Don Miguel Garcia and were using his death to covertly sway the two cartels into a drug war, all the while profiting from the emerging chaos created by the tumultuous instability.

The tugboat was en route to his Detachment area. They had more business to attend to on Lower Main Street, convincing potential clients to become loyal to their collaborate cause and not to either cartel. The recent murder of the tranny in the alley by Don Miguel Garcia was being used as an extortion influencer.

Ben returned to Captain Relic who confirmed his port-of-call. Ben mentioned that he had to contact a friend, a fellow deserter to pick him up. "Where's the best 24-hour coffee shop to meet, Relic?"

"I think that the only place open all night is King's Bakery on Fifth Avenue. Both the coffee and the grub are decent, and it's a comfortable place to hang out in the event that your friend has to drive a long distance. It's about a ten-minute walk from where I'll drop you off. I won't tie up, as I just want to put some distance between myself and the other two passengers. They always pay premium fares to keep me quiet. You'd do well to keep your distance also, my friend."

"Thanks, Relic. I very much appreciate the sage advice. I'll just arrange my ride." Ben texted Sue and Glen with his intel and ETA to the dockside.

'We'll be there as a reception party,' Glen texted back. 'Be prepared to be arrested with the other two. You've managed to amass more evidence on this case than anyone else. We may want to protect your identity for a future mission. BTW, Constable McLeod, we need to talk about protocol. I commend your initiative, BUT.'

Ben concluded from Glen's reference to his formal rank and surname that he was in for a disciplinary lecture from Sergeant Anderson. He could only prepare for this one-sided verbal encounter with the defence of being a probationary constable. He was more concerned with any backlash on Sue as his trainer and partner and confidant.

Chapter 18

"Hands up! Get on the ground! Hands Up! Get on the ground!" Commands rang out from behind, from both sides and in front of the suspects who were leading the hurried pace from the tugboat along the wharf, followed by Ben. Everywhere they looked uniformed RCMP officers were approaching with pistols drawn, pointed at them. Before they had an opportunity to assess their situation, these officers had forced them to the deck. Above the shouted orders, Ben could hear Relic's tugboat engine sing into high rpm as it sped away under concealment of darkness and a heavy mist that had imperceptibly shrouded the shoreline.

He had practiced takedowns in training. This was the first experience of an operational multiple arrest. It seemed weird to be on the receiving end of this agonising reality. Each arresting officer was simultaneously cuffing, searching, and providing a verbal warning of rights to their respective prisoner, including Ben.

He was impressed with the speed and effectiveness at which his colleagues had executed the restraining manoeuvre. He was less impressed with the knees that were grinding into the small of his back and neck. He then recognised his arresting officer as she assisted him to his feet. He had a renewed level of respect for the prowess of his partner.

All three were loaded into separate patrol cars. Ben gained a better appreciation for the limited space between the protective shield and the backbench seat. At the Detachment, they were searched again and lodged in separate cells with Ben in the middle. Sue remained in the cellblock and subsequently recited their rights once again. She then asked each prisoner individually if they understood. Ben confirmed that he did. The other two replied, "*No hablo inglés.*"

"*Un minute,*" Sue directed. She stepped to the doorway of the cellblock and asked for one of her colleagues to enter. "They say that they don't speak English, Hernandez. Can you translate?"

"*Entiemdes ingles,*" he enunciated in cultured Spanish.

"Yeah, we speak English," both grudgingly admitted.

"So you understood my warning," Sue confronted each individually.

"Yeah, I understand," each replied in response to her singular stare.

"Can you stay with the two Spanish prisoners, Hernandez, while I interview the other?"

Sue then unlocked Ben's cell door and instructed him to accompany her. They walked out of the cellblock and into the Detachment where Glen was waiting. His complexion still displayed traces of the makeup applied by Glenda.

As Sue removed his handcuffs, Glen approached to a congenial proximity. "I'd admonish you for violating protocol, Constable McLeod, but you're unaware of the protocol so I can't. I have to commend you instead. Outstanding job, Constable. I could not have pulled it off better myself. How would you like to join me on Commercial Crime once you have completed your probation?"

"Thank you, Sergeant," Ben chuckled under his breath. This was the second job offer of employment in as many weeks.

"If the interrogations reveal what I believe they will, you will be in for a Commanding Officer's Commendation for your initiative and potentially a more prestigious award for bravery. Your Detachment Commander will receive kudos for having one of his constables solve the drug cartel case and, in doing so, drive a holly stake into the heart of the drug war thereby stemming the flow of narcotics onto this turf. That's not to mention helping to solve the recent murder here."

"Thanks. But I couldn't have done it without my partner's stalwart assistance and your sagacious guidance," Ben humbly interjected.

"GIS and Major Crime are interviewing the suspects. Let's see what they come up with. I have briefed the Detachment Commander and your shift supervisor. I explained why they were not included in the beginning because your involvement at that juncture was routine, nothing out of the ordinary. They seemed to accept my explanation that the pace of the case only went exponential after you boarded the tugboat with the suspects."

Ben nodded in comfort of Glen's loyalty and support, acknowledging his wisdom and shrewd ability in balancing all the players and the politics of priorities.

"If you are to protect your informant, you will need to explain how you became aware of the suspects," Glen murmured in a more fatherly fireside tone. "Perhaps you just happened to be checking out the pubs in Sechelt on your days off when you overheard the suspects colluding. There was no time for you to call the Sechelt detachment because the suspects bolted for the tugboat by the time you realised what was unfolding."

Again, Ben nodded in humble appreciation of the wisdom being bestowed.

"Let's grab a coffee while we wait for the results from the GIS and Major Crime investigators," Glen suggested in a lighter, louder voice.

Ben huffed as he filled the cups for himself and his partner, while envisioning Relics stained coffee pot and brewed beans. He'd like to reconnect with the skipper some time when circumstances were more appropriate.

"What's with the knee in the kidneys, partner?"

"Just practicing my take-downs and hold-downs for my up-and-coming judo competition."

"You're good. No, you're great. There was no doubt in my mind that I wasn't going anywhere."

"Much appreciate the vote of confidence."

"Excuse me while I check in with Alejandra. We hadn't finished our first glass of wine before this all went down. I owe her a dedicated evening. Very much looking forward to boring night shifts with you."

As he texted, Sue recognised that her partner had been bitten with the bug for adventurous service. He had far greater potential and Glen could be his new mentor.

"Damn," Ben exclaimed. "My car is over in Sechelt. I need to get it somehow. When are our next days off?"

"No need to worry," the Detachment Commander piped up as he approached the familiar post-operational gathering around the coffee pot. He extended his hand to Ben. "Sergeant Anderson has briefed me on your involvement. I commend you on your initiative. I'll arrange for the helicopter to take you back to Sechelt to retrieve your car. Your days off will be extended an additional forty-eight hours due to this operational urgency. After we finish here, you head home and catch some sleep. One of the patrols will pick you up and take you to the landing pad. Now let's all head into the briefing room. I understand that the GIS and Major Crime investigators have completed their initial interviews."

Being caught together in cahoots was what broke this case. The investigators were confident that they would not be singing the same tune without that factor. The two suspects weren't sure but thought that there might be at least one if not a couple of other cartel agents working in the Sunshine Coast or on the east side of Vancouver Island. So, there was a need to maintain further vigilance and surveillance.

Proceeds of crime were being laundered through casinos and local motorcycle gangs, and cash transactions of valuable private collections of non-traceable property. They were light on specifics.

The suspects would not be charged with any offence. Instead, they would be released as confidential informants to return to their respective cartels, knowing that their confessions had been recorded on CCTV. They were very much aware that if their partnership was disclosed, they would both be hunted down and murdered in the most vicious manner, akin to the slashing of the female in the alley. This would be a signal to others contemplating disloyalty.

The reference to at least one if not a couple of other cartel agents in the region caught Ben's attention. Alejandra might still be in danger. Different scenarios skittered about his synaptic circuits, revealing a myriad of disturbing consequences. What would Sherlock Holmes contemplate? Was it this elementary, Watson?

Ben texted Alejandra with his tentative ETA and asked if they could meet at the same pub.

Chapter 19

Ben's eyes traced her every movement as she approached the booth where they had sat last evening. He was entranced once again with her mere presence. She was a lady in the truest sense whose natural beauty and radiance would glow like the golden sun in any shrouded ambiance, particularly where sheer elegance was revered. Paris's greatest gift to the world is its beautiful alluring women. Alejandra is an honorary Parisian, a captivating patrician of the Champs-Élysées.

"Two glasses of Pinot Noire?" the server suggested.

"Make it a bottle?" Ben responded without averting his eyes from Alejandra's affectionate attention whilst seeking her accord.

There was a meditative moment before she responded and, like her rendezvous consort, she maintained her continuous contemplation. Her nod and tender smile confirmed his selection.

Looking closer, he tried to interpret the veiled message in her deep brown eyes all the while maintaining a purposeful explorative pause. He watched her carefully for a reaction but there was only a continued period of eloquent silence. He searched for feelings, for the story, because there was more truth in story than detail in fact, and story would lead him to the truth. Then there it was, a rueful flinch, followed by a rapid recovery. There was regret for goodness gone awry. He had time. He would have the evening, the night to explore, to evaluate, to gauge, to reassess.

The mood of the pub and Alejandra's scent triggered thoughts of last evening's ephemeral encounter. Something just didn't settle with him, in retrospect. The boy from Trail had spent a lifetime honing his skills to become a professional observer, a proficient judge of character, of motivation, with an adept eye, tutored by the best, the pragmatic Sir Arthur Conan Doyle. And reinforced by many others, most recently Sue and Ralph and Glen, and Captain Relic, and even the two suspects with their gnarled glares.

Touching hands and caressing fingers seemed natural, as if practiced to proficiency in another lifetime when circumstances beyond their control separated them like Romeo and Juliette, with a potential promise of a later reunion, perhaps just as fleeting.

They paused on their promenade along the beach walkway. In unison, they embraced and gazed intimately into each other's eyes with evocative valentine invitations.

"*Eres hermosa*, you are beautiful," Ben whispered.

"*Besa me*, kiss me," Alejandra murmured. "*Te amo*, I love you."

Without hesitation, his response was passionately avowed. "*Yo también te amo*, I love you too."

On the short drive to her apartment, she snuggled into his now familiar scent and form.

She had never experienced it, felt it, sensed it, witnessed it. Instead only read about it, dreamed it, imagined it, this tenderness, this gentleness, this decency, this caring.

In her nightmares that were as violently vivid today as ever, she would attempt to escape the stifling heat and the acrid smells and the numbing noise and the stinging smoke of the sleazy nightclubs. At the same time, talentless girls with discolouring hair and mascara-stained eyes would be mindlessly undulating on a mucus-stained pole and a beer-covered floor while disingenuously caressing the distorted silhouettes of stripped naked juvenile bodies.

An executive of the drug trade had dragged her away into a life marginally more sanitary but infrequently less abusive. He had never noticed her as a person. There was fabricated assurance of a temporary monopoly of unrealistic love, or more often just an intoxicated repugnant and persistently abusive bed.

She was intuitive and strategic enough to take advantage of influenced serendipity of the drug lord lifestyle, offering more freedom to ponder opportunities and stealthily plan her clandestine egress. Contrived chance provided better odds than the role of the dice at a crap table that she knew all too well. Ironically, it was these kaleidoscopic events from her past that provided her with the requisite experiences to analyse and execute with success an escape from the confinement of her own Stalag Luft III. But that was then. Today was now. The bipolar-like world of incessant fear and intermittent interludes of armistice with sporadic narcotic-like flash backs of fairy tale affection were immediate.

She gently lowered her head back onto Ben's muscular chest and reached out with eyes wide open to touch the fantasy, the fairy tale story once again. She was a creature of God, born into conflict, self-educated by instinct. Hers was a journey of sequential episodes, as if ascending an escalator to somewhere, but pausing on each anonymous level to look up ever searching through the mist to where she was going, before she looked down into the infected fog of where she had been.

For now, she closed her eyes against those horrid memories in an effort to avoid yesterday and create some reason for tomorrow while in Ben's reassuring embrace. She might only be in a dream, another dream, like the others, but escapism brought relief, if only temporarily. He was in her dreams and hopefully she was in his dreams too. It was enough to survive another night, alone. Alone without abuse was progress. A night with Ben brought faint hope. She shivered in expectation, overshadowed with trepidation of omnipresent recollections of trite clichés, and insincerity and impermanence.

He listened to her breathing and monitored her heartbeat. At one moment, they would be calm and peaceful, then transformed into distressed thrashing of her legs and arms as if frantically fending off unimaginable assailants with their sweaty groping paws. This erratic enactment would be accentuated with inaudible mumbling of unresponsive demands.

Ever so gentle caressing of her contorted facial expressions seemed to return her to a state of tranquillity if only transitory. Greek mythology proposed that the beauty of Helen of Troy could launch a fleet of a thousand ships. Alejandra's beauty during these serene moments could launch a thousand fleets each with a thousand ships. He wanted to be by her side, with her, forever. But … damn …

During her uninterrupted peaceful periods, he concentrated on the soothing silence of her being, serenaded by the metronome cadence of waves on the incoming tide. The moonlight cascading through the skylight and bay window softly illuminated the loft. He ran his eye inquisitively around. Her one room abode was clean, fastidiously tidy, almost obsessively so. The trappings of domesticity were sparse yet far from Spartan. They were of superior quality, certainly beyond the range of a transitory café baker's negligible remuneration, in contrast. These fleeting images accompanied him into his slumber and Neverland of Peter Pan and Wendy.

He reached over but felt only faint warmth where she had laid. His semi-conscious senses were being aroused and caressed by the aroma of brewing java beans and baking muffins. If this was a dream, he did not want to awaken to the reality of the day that would have him driving back to the island, alone.

He felt her before he saw her.

"Good morning," she greeted him with a sensuous searching hug and an extended gentle kiss. "What do you take in your coffee?"

"You … and two cream as succulent as your touch."

"Two cream coming up. Banana and chocolate chip muffins will be out of the oven in three minutes. We can explore other options after breakfast."

He subtly huffed as he observed her over the rim of his second cup of steaming coffee. Under her alluring beauty lay potentially wary mysteries that needed to be brought to the surface and discussed within the context of whatever their relationship might become. He lingered in reserved silence.

"What do you want me to say?"

Ben discerningly pursed his inquiring lips and quietly nodded with an encouraging gentle gesture as he pointed with his eyes at some of her affluent possessions.

"What about us?" she responded apprehensively after an extended sip of coffee that provided a postponing interval.

"What about us?" Ben repeated returning the volley.

"I agree. Us is a function of all this ... and more. Where would you like me to begin? There is a lot of baggage, history, veiled narrations. Some I'm not so proud of."

"The philosopher, Soren Kienkegaard said that life can only be understood backwards, but it must be lived forward. When we were at UVic, you alluded to extant events in Cancun, with your family. Why not start there?"

"Do you really want to hear all the sordid details?"

Ben nodded assuredly.

She inhaled deeply raising her stare methodically to the ceiling and then exhaled as slowly as she lowered her head before re-engaging. "I grew up in a neighbourhood ravaged by the drug wars. There were mangy cowering canines and flea-infested feral felines amidst hordes of roaming free-range rats. The pungent stench of death and disease were brought on by a dearth of education and ubiquitous corruption. The swarms of fat flies gave evidence to the number of dead bloating bodies that they fed on and length of time they lay in the sweltering hovels of the slums, and the gutters adjacent to the doorways without doors."

Alejandra paused to gather her emotions, the first of several that punctuated the candidness of her graphic recollections.

"I never knew my father. My mother told me in one of her infrequent quasi-lucid drunken stupors that he didn't know that I existed because she wasn't sure which one he might have been. That was life in the barrio."

Ben starred in stunned silence. He had heard second and third hand stories of what was related as unfortunate souls, but they were gullibly distant and taciturnly void of the poignant pain of the first hand raconteur.

"I learned to survive with my wits and God's grace. Early on, I decided to leave revenge to providence, and to others because, if I didn't, I would be dragged into the inferno of purgatory never to surface again. I received my formal education from the nuns who ran a school. Sister Catherine saw promise in me and constantly reminded me that I had great potential. She was a rare realist in service to her mostly disillusioned flock who were as spent and broken as their souls. But she provided me with unwavering guidance and helped me map out an escape plan."

Her eyes dropped, her voice faltered, her lips paled. Ben sensed that she was on the cusp of revealing a deeply agonising tormenting episode. He leaned into her not wanting to miss any detail she reticently committed to share.

"There was no work that wasn't drug related. So you did what you had to do to survive, including muling for the drug lords, and being mauled and molested by the addicted parasites who frequented the festering filth of the gutters and lewdness of the immoral back alleys."

He was silenced by the images. He swallowed a suffocating emotion. He sat frozen in muted support. He walked beside her as she sobbed with the revelation of the sordid details that she had dredged up but never before divulged with such depth of probity.

She was being brutally honest in hopes of clearing away garbage that might get in the way of any potential relationship that they might have.

Chapter 20

Alejandra admitted to continued connection with the Cancun cartel, even today. She was just an informant. "I rarely tell the truth, the whole truth, and nothing but the truth. I just give enough to satisfy their needs so they will pay me. Forever is a very long time, but drugs have been around forever. You can start with shaman drugs for early cultural ailments. When the motivation is profit and not healing, violence erupts. I provide information on competing cartels to prevent local violence. Yes, the Cancun cartel can be vicious. God knows, I've experienced that myself. My decisions are for the lesser of the evils."

"You are paid how?"

"They make deposits to a Swiss bank account. It is my private retirement savings plan. You might find this surprising to hear, but Sister Catherine taught me about having offshore bank accounts. She warned that the corrupt tentacles of the drug lords reached into the banks in the Grand Caymans. I had to move beyond their groping grasp."

That titbit of news caused a reticent chuckled response from Ben who facetiously thought that he might want to hire Sister Catherine as a financial consultant.

"They don't know where I live exactly, just somewhere on the Pacific Northwest between Oregon and Alaska because I provide information relating to these locations. I have a plebeian lifestyle, so my needs are simple, humble. That was my life growing up in the barrio and I like it that way. But I have acquired a taste for quality, as you have noticed."

"If I gave you false information, would you pass that along?" Ben inquired, all the while thinking of the strategic implications and balancing of objectives.

Alejandra got up to refresh their mugs of coffee. It offered an interlude to consider his question. "Yes, subject to," she self-consciously admitted. "Yes, I need to report monthly or on other occasions when circumstances pose an immediate threat to operations. Subject to, because I'm trying to figure out how I can make a clear break from the cartel and start a new life with a new identity."

Ben reflected on his first formal meeting with Glen in the hotel room that propelled him into this arena. He needed to hang out with Glen more to master the art and science of the equilibrium from the expert. Glen would be more readily available to him if Alejandra could help him solve the money laundering case.

"What do you know about money laundering?"

"Casinos have been a common venue for money laundering for decades and still are. Becoming more popular today is the purchase and sale of incredibly valuable collectable merchandise and moving money through small legitimate businesses."

"Who benefits?"

"Let me back up a bit. My cartel has some dirty cops and prosecutors on the payroll. They also have their hooks into some senior government people in immigration."

They all benefit significantly to varying degrees.

Ben's quizzical expression prompted Alejandra to elaborate.

"That's just a fact. I don't know names but they are here on the West Coast in Vancouver and on the Island. There are also some higher up people in universities who recruit potential teachers in the education faculties and schools of business."

"Do you know how they're recruited?"

"An increasing number of students are from Asia, China, India and the Middle East. They are recruited before they come to Canada. If they agree, then the recruiters help them to get their student visas. The federal government has a program to increase Asian students. If they get even a diploma, then they are on the fast track to getting a landed immigrant card and then a Canadian citizenship. They can then bring in their entire extended family. It's a good deal just to traffic the proceeds of drugs."

"There are border security and police whose primary jobs are to catch and prosecute."

"Yes but more and more of these officials, particularly police, are being diverted towards terrorism enforcement. That's a big scam considering the actual threat. Cops like these jobs because it's an easy assignment, a scam for some, so they don't have to do much and they get all the new enforcement toys to play with. When asked, they simply say that it's secret so they can't reveal any details. They are chasing the boogiemen and women, most of whom don't exist. As for the prosecution, the government lawyers want the really high-profile cases so they can get promoted. They don't take on these little time-consuming low-profile cases that won't bring them any glory. If you want resources, then manipulate the media. That's really easy because the myopic scumarazzi paparazzi only report sensationalism. One other point. There is a vice president of one of the big bank branches on the payroll also."

"OK, so how is the money actually laundered? We're talking hundreds of thousands of dollars even many millions in small denominations, mostly twenties and fifties."

"Yes but these amounts are in the big cities like Vancouver and Toronto and Montreal. In smaller communities like the Sunshine Coast and the Island, they function by doing a high volume of smaller operations. For example, you buy a couple of pubs and pad the books by depositing a consistent top-up to your daily sales by five thousand. It's small stuff so there aren't the police resources to investigate even if it is picked up in audits. There are lots of small businesses like pubs or used car lots that operate this way. The pub where we met does business this way. The VP of the bank that I mentioned facilitates these transactions. He or she greases the wheels so to speak for deposits."

Ben concluded that Alejandra was telling the truth. He knew from training that successful money launderers slipped the money into legitimate businesses like pubs with a consistent amount each day so as not to attract attention. That got it into the legitimate economy by obscuring the source. They would then make legitimate withdrawals. It was the classic triad of placement, layering and integration.

They got away with it by not being greedy, keeping a very low profile, being a conservative pillar of the community, attending church, donating to community charity events but not too much, driving a four-door mid-sized car and never speeding.

In contrast, it was greed that brought some biker gangs to the attention of police. The intimidating antics of the gang members caused citizens to feel fearful. So the citizens called their politicians who told the police to put a damper on the crime so the citizens would feel safe and re-elect the politicians. It's all about keeping the customer satisfied.

Ben starred at her from a self-imposed detached distance analysing the sheer volume and detail of her admissions. He had to clarify a nagging question. "You seem to know a great deal for an uneducated naïve girl from the barrio."

Alejandra locked eyes with a defensive defiant stare. "Sister Catherine reminded me over and over that if I were to survive in that hell, I needed to know more about the devil than the devil knew about himself. Knowledge is power. I spent many hours patiently observing and listening from behind the deceptive veil of the lucid curtains and coherent bed sheets. As you just astutely noted, I am more than an innocent girl from the barrio. I was dragged into that malicious immoral world, blinded by ignorance. I am executing my strategic escape on the back of the two-headed tiger. My knowledge is my passport to freedom. It will be my execution warrant if they find out how much I actually know. Believe me when I say that there are no limits to their venomous commandments. My life is in your hands Constable Ben McLeod, and now that you know, the signing of my execution warrant will be the deliverance and sounding of your death knell also."

With that revelation, Ben acknowledged the stark reality that they were wedded, both committed to and condemned by these vows of secrecy.

"You need to be especially wary and vigilant for internal threats, Ben," Alejandra cautioned. "There are some dirty cops and lawyers on the take. Somewhere on the coast, there is a senior sergeant and at least one cop in the drug section who are on the cartel payroll. They are in cahoots with one of the government lawyers, a female prosecutor. You can't trust everyone. I'll do my best to find out more."

Ben was correct in his initial analysis of Alejandra when he briefed Sue. Alejandra is a product of *las calles* in the barrio, a survivor of that subsistent vicious world. Sue was also correct in her initial assessment of Ben that he would ultimately make the correct decisions, like Sherlock Homes. Alejandra was correct in her initial assessment that she and Ben were from two different worlds and the probability of them establishing a forever relationship, being a permanent fixture, was very low. But maybe there might be a way. Alejandra had agreed to be a double agent, an informant for him.

He needed time to think about the intelligence that she had just provided, what he would do with it, and their evolving relationship. He refilled his coffee, walked over to the bay window and stared at the vista not really concentrating on anything in particular. He then gazed over at Alejandra who was still sitting at the table with her head lowered. Her hands were spread out as if in an apologetic gesture soliciting unconditional forgiveness.

One of her revelations was now gnawing at him, her disclosure that there was a senior sergeant on the take. Sue had previously mentioned that they couldn't trust everyone. Alejandra just reinforced that. But was the crooked cop Glen? Sue introduced him in the hotel room as a good guy, someone they could trust. But could he, could they. He needed to talk with Sue and soon.

He wanted to be close to Alejandra to support her more than ever, but knew that he needed to keep his distance so as not to be distracted, and to protect her. Yet the ache of leaving her was starting to take a toll on his ability to remain objective. She was alluring and wary and she was presenting both to a fault.

The paralysis of protection from years of pain, of imprisoning her love, kept her limp arms from reaching out. Her throat was tight with the emotion she had been feeling. She tried to smile confidently but it didn't work. Instead she canted her head to one side, raised her half lower lip to cover her upper lip and looked at him closely, then took a slow deep breath.

"So, where are we? Where are Alejandra and Ben?" she timidly inquired with a shy shallow little girl voice, almost pleading for reassurance that there was a possibility of a future.

Despite the fact that he looked apprehensive and hesitant, she felt hopeful as he stood sentinel assuredly presenting the courageous image of a Teutonic knight weighing options and debating decisions. She had not previously noticed the gold signet ring of nobility that he wore on his left hand steadfastly announcing honour and unwavering loyalty to a deeper duty, a heraldic calling, a pious vow like a wedding band should, but with increasing frequency does not.

He stared out the bay window again, this time at the motionless gulls perched on abandoned deadheads and the momentary calmness of the changing tide, while formulating his response. He needed to reciprocate the agonising honesty.

"I don't know. I just don't know. I know where I would like us to be. Last night was an indisputable confirmation of that. But we are two worlds apart, you and I. We currently have this relationship and we will always have this relationship, even if it is just joyful memories of what was last night and the fanciful imaginings of what could have been under different circumstances."

Alejandra overheard his murmur with an innocent invitation. "We'll always have Paris."

"Humphrey Bogart and Ingrid Bergman in one of the final scenes of Casablanca," she recounted with a subdued intention.

"You've seen the movie?"

"One of my much-loved all-time classics. If I've seen it once, I've seen it a hundred and one times."

Ben smiled in sentimental reflection of the countless occasions that he sat in front of his TV screen captivated by that and so many other magical scenes.

"Want to watch it one more time when I'm over next? I've got it recorded and tagged as one of my favourites."

Alejandra's eyes sparkled and her face glowed at the prospects of spending a secluded one hour and forty-minute presentation together. Reassuring affectionate warmth calmed her as she reflected on his words – when I'm over next.

In the serenity of the meditative moment and the tenderness of their mutual embrace, he became acutely aware that she was both his forbidden fruit and his passion fruit. He knew what the dispassionate Sherlock Holmes would say and what the political Glen Anderson would say. But what would intuitive strategic Ben McLeod say? Is it a case of either or, either Alejandra or his career? Or is it a possibility of both and, both Alejandra and his career? Like Winnie the Pooh, he would have to ponder over a pot of honey.

After cleaning up the breakfast dishes, they descended the back wrought iron staircase to the secluded parking space and his car.

"Do you know how much I do not want to leave you?" Ben sighed as he encircled her waist and drew her to him. Parting is sweet sorrow as Shakespeare wrote. At this moment, parting simply sucks big time, he genuinely lamented.

"Not half as much as I do not want you to leave. In the off chance that you might forget last night, I've placed the rest of the muffins in this bag that I crocheted for you. I embroidered your name on the cover. Don't eat them all at once. Save at least one for a late snack this evening. Remember that they're far better fresh."

"Thank you, *mi querida* – my dearest. Like the baker, far better fresh."

"You could have them hot out of the oven every morning with freshly brewed coffee served in bed with a caressing hug, if you stayed."

"Let me communicate my deepest desire in braille, my beautiful Mata Hari," he endearingly traced his index finger over her moist trembling lips trailed by a kiss of devoted passion that he had never experienced before.

Their parting embrace was inclusive of what needed to be said. No words could bring greater clarity. Yet more, much more, needed to be worked out. Ben could still sense a ting of a remorseful thread almost imperceptibly tugging at her past, a bygone life impacted by decisions she reluctantly made under the duress of inconceivable circumstances analogous to the insanity of Dante's inferno, but now profoundly regretted.

Always was a very long time. Alejandra's past was her past and was part of her present, and always would be. He needed to be conscious of but not biased by that unambiguous stark reality as he stepped into the unknown battle space of a savage merciless drug war, strewn with IEDs and landmines by seemingly unseen callous combatants as ruthless as any he had encountered in Afghanistan.

Ben was abruptly struck by the veracity and implications of Alejandra's world, the cartel hellhole into which Kaplanski had voluntarily descended, hopefully with eyes wide open and with all senses on full alert.

Chapter 21

Ben's message to Sue was terse but clear. 'We need to talk soonest. Will meet you at your place.'

No sooner had he sent it than he received a text from Alejandra marked Urgent: Stalin Purge. 'My employer is extremely agitated with obliqueness of death of their agent. As a result, they are conducting a Stalinist purge of anyone who might be a snitch or anyone who may have infiltrated its bastions, specifically new arrivals to their world who might be undercover cops. There is a Russian connection, a hacker by the name of Sergei who was recruited to engage in cyber warfare against the other cartels. Sergei has used his talents to infiltrate primarily US but also other law enforcement agencies. Apparently, there is a Canadian connection so they warned me to use extra caution. I strongly suggest you do the same.'

***

"Got your cryptic message, partner. You're not looking like a happy camper. I figured that you'd be all smiles after a few days taking in the sights of Sechelt. Instead, you're looking like you just walked out of an exam that you hadn't studied for. Coffee is on. Let's chat."

"Do you remember warning me about corruption within the Force and government, and the need to be very careful?"

"Yes. Why do you ask?"

"My source reiterated your warning almost verbatim. She said that there was a police sergeant on her boss's payroll. She didn't have a name or any other information. How well do you know Glen and how much do you really trust him?"

Sue tightened her lips and slowly moved her head from left to right and back again all the time meeting Ben's stare. "I first met him when I was on course at the Canadian Police College. My intuition suggested that he was one of the white-hatted good guys. When we met again at the Bayview Hotel with Ralph, my gut still confirmed that he could be trusted. I'm picking up some doubt from you?"

Ben's fingers slowly circled the rim of the coffee mug. "I've been mulling over this intel all the way back from Sechelt, carefully analysing all the factors. If the implications weren't so serious, I wouldn't have thought twice. I think that I still trust him but now not one hundred percent sure."

"Maybe ninety-nine-point-nine-eight percent in this game of cat and mouse is as good as it gets."

"Let's put it into context of another piece of intel that I received. Do you know a female crown prosecutor? My source indicated that this person is also on the take and is helping with money laundering operations by not prosecuting certain cases that land on her desk. Like the sergeant, my source had no further information."

"There are several female crowns in the Province. I'm not surprised to hear this but for now we just need to file it."

"A third bit of intel to add to the cauldron," Ben offered as he slowly sipped his coffee. "There is a vice president with one of the big bank branches who is helping one of the money launderers with deposits of dirty money. Like the sergeant and the crown prosecutor, my source has no further information but will find out more if at all possible."

"I have a better understanding why you aren't a totally happy camper. And why we need to talk. Good work. I have some anti-acid medication if you need any."

Ben sat staring at his coffee contemplating Sue's offer of hyper-acidity medication.

"I sense that there is more."

Ben slowly looked up, huffed slightly, and after a troublesome pause he nodded. "On my way back, my source sent me an urgent text." Ben showed Sue the message under the subject 'Urgent – Stalinist purge.'

Sue read and re-read the text. "My suggestion, and you can disagree with me. We pass along the Stalinist purge intel to Glen. If Glen is the white-hatted good sergeant, we may well save Kaplanski from being beat up or worse. If we don't and Glen is one of the good guys and Kaplanski gets killed, we will have his blood on our hands. If we do pass this intel along to Glen and he turns out to be one of the black hats and Kaplanski gets wiped out, we still have some blood on our hands but we expose a dirty cop."

Ben squinted and wrinkled his face as he warily contemplated the options presented. "Passing this intel along to Glen immediately is our only choice. We just pray that Glen is a white-hatted good guy. I think that we also mention the Russian hacker, Sergei, as he may be onto Kaplanski. Until such time as we can be one hundred percent sure that Glen is a good guy, we hold back on the other intel regarding the crown prosecutor and the bank VP."

Sue nodded in agreement. "Apart from that Mrs Lincoln, how was your evening at the opera?" Sue uttered in her best black humour.

"Like the comparison, partner. Apart from that, Sechelt was awesome." He smiled contentedly but with a reserved hiatus that Sue missed as she refilled the mugs of coffee.

***

"I shouldn't be but continue to be impressed, amazed with the quality and complexity of the intelligence that the two of you bring to this file," Glen admitted after being briefed by Sue and Ben.

"We may be able to access additional information regarding the money laundering operations on the coast." Ben added, "not sure when but we'll let you know soonest. I can confirm that it is international, beyond Canada and the US, reaching into Asia but primarily into Europe."

Glen grinned that Ben was becoming renowned for his extremely tentative pronouncement. "Intel has confirmed that the Central American cartels have embraced the international marketplace with a 21st century global perspective. With their expanded business stratagem, they have been instrumental in establishing a tenuous yet maturing relationship with a growing number of visionary partners, including some strategic thinkers within the hierarchy of a select few offshore biker gangs. They have also gone high tech. This is money laundering through drug trafficking at a global level, taking advantage of nefarious trans-national parties, including contemporary terrorist groups like ISIS and more traditional organisations such as The Fourth Reich, the benefactor of the Nazi Third Reich and their stolen treasures. Interpol is doing its best to investigate, infiltrate and coordinate enforcement but the bad guys outnumber the good guys in boots on the ground and technical resources."

"I got a sense of this while in Afghanistan by observing late night activities, specifically the comings and goings of night flights of US C141 Starlifters into Kandahar airport with special black ops forces. This was hush-hush stuff that no one talked about openly except those few who had situational awareness. Americans were very rank conscious and, as a result, were perceived as being arrogant. They never saw Canadians as equal partners, so if you played dumb like Colombo, the TV detective character, you could find out all sorts of information."

"Interesting!" Glen commented. "The world has and continues to change at an exponential rate. The bad guys are focused on the 22nd century while some within the RCMP are still referencing 1873 and the Great March West of 1874 to Fort Walsh in the Cypress Hills of Saskatchewan. The bad guys operate under just one rule and that is, there are no rules. Policing under democracies, in contrast, are restricted by volumes of constricting codes, laws and regulations."

Ben reflected on those images of clandestine night flights and the balaclava attired black ops quasi-military personnel and other black-hooded or blindfolded passengers who disembarked never to be seen again. But he was mostly intrigued with the myriad of antennae that protruded from atop security instillations behind multiple layers of barbed wire and non-descript heavily armed guards. He had heard rumours about similar activities in off-the-map places with names like Dodge City near Tuzla in the Former Republic of Yugoslavia. These stories had tweaked his interest but he was too far down the food chain of the hierarchy to verify any details gleaned from quiet sources.

Within the context of drug cartel involvement in international crime that Glen was describing, it all started to fall into place. He was connecting the dots where before there had just been fog banks. What he and Sue were doing on night patrol wouldn't even be a blip on that radar screen. The murder of the tranny was a serendipitous springboard into this other world that Glen was tiptoeing through, and offering Sue and him a rare and enticing but potentially deadly glimpse, akin to the lethal consequences of Alejandra's intelligence.

Ben became reflective, pensive, and analytical. He pondered whether Alejandra had experienced such a menacing ill-omened apparition and, as a result, had chosen to run in the opposite direction, to the Sunshine Coast. Was this all a Mad Hatter's trip down the vexing rabbit hole that Alejandra had travelled in her own beguiling Wonderland of Alice?

For now, their focus would continue to be on the extant mundane night patrols and the mysterious movements of the white Toyota in and out of the parking lot of the Bayview Hotel monitored by the night auditor.

Glen looked at Ben inquisitively. "A tangential question? At the briefing after the arrests, the Detachment Commander referenced your linguistic talents."

"Yes, I was embarrassed with his pronouncement."

"You speak more than Spanish?"

"That's correct. I am fluent in Russian and German, in addition to Spanish, although my German is rusty."

Glen continued to gaze at Ben, tilting his head, raising his shoulders, and presenting his open hands palms up as a prompt for explanation.

"My grandparents on my mother's side emigrated from Russia. My mother's first tongue is Russian so we spoke

Russian and English at home. I spent many summers with my grandparents where we spoke nothing but Russian."

"And German," Glen prompted.

"I'm a military brat. My father was posted to Berlin, Germany twice as a military attaché. We lived in a German community. I mentioned that my German is rusty because I learned to speak it from the German kids I hung out with. I leaned German grammar in school but it was pretty basic. Before you ask, yes, I also speak BC French as opposed to Quebec French."

"You speak five languages!" Glen confirmed in astonishment.

"Yes," Ben sheepishly replied as if that was the normal.

"And you seem to have superior knowledge of and interest in world affairs!" Glen added.

"I guess so. That was conversation around the dinner table at home. You may not be aware that Canadian military attachés were informal spies because Canada did not officially have a CIA or MI6 foreign spy service. My father's job was to gather intelligence after the Berlin wall had been abandoned by Moscow, and Gorbachev had introduced perestroika and glasnost. Berlin was awash with ex-East Germans, many of whom had been employed by the KGB as neighbourhood spies, better known as snitches. Some were actual spies working for the FSB, the successor to the KGB. New wineskin, same old wine. As I said, dinner conversations were intriguing especially when my father entertained guests from different agencies."

"After these files are closed, Ben, we need to sit down and talk about your career. With tongue in cheek, I asked you before if you would like to work with me in Commercial Crime. With all due respect for general duty policing at the detachment level, and even Commercial Crime, you have got far superior potential."

"I will, Glen. Thanks for the offer. I'd like to speak with Sue first and get her advice before I make any decisions."

Chapter 22

"Ralph, you there, hiding in the back?"

"I'm here as always, Sue. Haven't seen you for a while. Missed our intellectual interludes. What's up?"

"Apologise. It's been a tad busy lately."

"Java beans are brewing. Was able to wangle a few fresh donuts out of Joan at King's Bakery."

"Anything worth watching on CCTV?" Ben inquired.

"Just the normal. The two guys who called in with their credit cards showed up. They were just a couple of Ministry of Advanced Education blokes from Victoria, so didn't notify you."

"Has the white Toyota made its initial visitation? Any change in routine?"

"It was here about two hours ago. It slowed down to navigate around the traffic cone, as did all the other regulars. Should be back any time now."

"Mind if we park our chariot of fire off to the side, out of sight? We don't want to spook the clients."

"Be my guest. You can sit in the office with me to keep out of sight. The driver usually glances over at me when he slides in. We can watch the entertainment on the CCTV monitor in the office."

Before they could finish their first cups, the Toyota quietly cruised past the cone and into its favourite spot.

"Let's just give it a few minutes to settle in before we sashay on down for a little discrete surveillance and follow up conversation," Sue suggested.

"Sounds like a plan," Ben leisurely agreed. "That will give me time to finish the last dregs and wash the glaze off my fingers. Mighty fine grub and drink," he motioned to

Ralph with a smile. "One of these shifts I'll tell you a story about dregs of coffee."

"You cover the passenger side while I take the driver."

Ben nodded in concurrence.

Sue rapped on the window, which resulted in the driver lowering it. "Good evening, sir," Sue barked.

"How can I help you?"

"Have noticed that over the past few weeks you have been parking here twice. The first time you have a female passenger. The second time you seem to be alone, like now. Can you explain your actions?"

The driver grinned as he passed Sue a letter signed by the Dean of Social Work from the University of British Columbia. It explained that he was a student in the Master's Degree program. He was conducting research into legal aid and other social services to those who need them the most but access them the least.

Sue returned the letter and the documentation after recording the information and drawing the driver's attention to her partner standing by the passenger's side of the car.

"I interview homeless people who populate the world from dusk to dawn and record their stories. Some I interview on the streets where they live or in an all-night café like King's Bakery."

"Why here in the parking lot?" Ben asked.

"This Hotel parking lot is relatively safe because there is a night auditor and the hotel has recently installed a CCTV surveillance system. I like that from a safety perspective. Some clients feel safe here because they are not comfortable being seen with a stranger anywhere downtown. Suffice to say, you can't do this research during the daytime in pristine offices like the Pan Pacific Centre in downtown Vancouver. So my car becomes my office. The second time I drive here, I sit and listen to the recordings of the interviews and make notes." He showed Sue and Ben his iPad. "This way I have a better chance of relocating these people and completing a follow up interview should I need to."

"You keep a record of the interviewees," Ben interjected through the passenger window that was part way down.

"I keep a list of all those I interview as a record. If you would like to verify the names, I can give you a copy with the consent forms that some of the interviewees sign. Those people of the night who do not sign are just too fearful of people of the day life. I just record their names, often just their street pseudo names. As you might appreciate if you work a lot of night shifts, it takes a long time to gain their confidence. I also keep a copy of my notes on the iCloud. I need to ensure that there are lots of back-ups for audit trail purposes."

"Mind if I verify your interviews with some of your clients?"

"Be my guest. I'll be here for another week or so."

"Did you have an opportunity to interview the female who was murdered before she met her demise?"

"I don't think so. I say that because I don't know who she was. She would be the type of person we would want to help. Perhaps if the government had a night office here, she might not be dead."

"Possibly so," Sue replied. "Would you do something for me?"

"Sure."

"Could you drop into the Detachment tomorrow and provide them with a copy of your letter with your ID?"

The driver looked at Sue with a deer-in-the-headlights stunned stare. "The Dean sent a letter to the CO E Division to that effect. I know because I prepared the letter, was present when she signed it, and then I mailed it personally."

"Thanks and apologies if we messed up. I will follow up tomorrow also. Have a pleasant night."

"Thoughts partner," Sue questioned as they made their way back to Ralph's nocturnal abode.

"Sounds legit. Not picking up any suspicious vibes. He seems to have covered off all the bases for research protocol, except perhaps dropping into the detachment to verify that we have a copy of the Dean's letter. But if it was never an issue in the past, he would have no reason to think otherwise. I wouldn't be surprised if our new support person just filed the letter without first checking with her supervisor. In the immortal words of one of my favourite cartoon characters, Foghorn J. Leghorn, in referring to his young nephew, 'I say that boy is as bright as a wet bag on ice'."

"Love the analogy! We have all the credential information we need. I'll check on the pony express in the morning if you call UBC."

"All appears to be OK, Ralph," Sue reported. "Will confirm tomorrow if there is anything of concern."

"I'll pack the traffic cone back into the trunk," Ben offered. "Like these same old, same old, cut and paste night patrol reports. A small distraction like this adds a little spice to the otherwise bland soup."

"Got a second cup, Ralph? Will pass on the second donut though as I am still in training for my black belt judo competition."

***

"UBC confirmed his research."

"Foghorn Leghorn's relative did just file the letter as we suspected! You have to wonder about public service commission hiring standards. Standards may be an oxymoron."

"Need to brief you on a conversation I just had with Alejandra regarding money laundering. She wanted to talk as opposed to texting because she has a feeling that her e-world has been hacked, not that there ever was much confidentiality."

"OK. Let's mount up."

"Alejandra said that there is a high volume of smaller amounts of cash, mostly just several thousand dollars being laundered through professional book buyers and sellers known as the antiquarian world. Some first edition, first print autographed books are worth tens of thousands of dollars, a few into the hundreds of thousands. Apparently, a copy of Robinson Crusoe recently sold for fifteen thousand dollars."

Sue whistled in amazement. "Nice hobby craft."

"My thoughts exactly. There are antiquarians worldwide. So there is no shortage of either supply or demand in this marketplace."

Sue tilted her head and raised her shoulders. "The local market?"

"On the west coast, Seattle hosts an annual event attended by international antiquarian book dealers. There are above the table public transactions and there are under the table private dealings at these events."

"How are the books moved?"

"Apparently, it's easy. Customs inspectors never notice books on the discrete library shelves of private yachts that cruise the west coast from Canada to Mexico. This is a very clean process, very quiet, very profitable, and virtually impossible to trace because books are not registered in any public or private directories. Christmas is the high-volume season for moving money and merchandise because most cops are on holidays at home with their families. Those who are supposed to be working are also at home, just on call. If they actually are on patrol, they make fewer routine traffic stops."

"Accurate assessment."

"Alejandra said that re-runs of the Beachcombers are being shown on EU television. As a result, wealthy Europeans are coming to visit the Sunshine Coast and Gibsons. It's a tourist attraction that the local Chamber of Commerce is effectively promoting. Some are bringing select valuable books from their private antiquarian collections with them to meet the underground demand. Some of these Europeans have financial interest in EU style pubs which are being used to launder money also. In addition, single-term exchange students are bringing in valuable books with aid from some college and university administrators and Deans who have tapped into this very lucrative second income stream without T4 slips. These students are paid a handsome sum for their efforts. It subsidises their education, and some go home with money in their pockets."

"When you prostitute yourself for the almighty dollar, you abrogate your integrity, that ability to steadfastly adhere to moral standards," Sue muttered. "Time to have a chin wag with Glenda."

"Case one, the murder, solved. Case two, the drug importation, solved. Now case three, Glen's money laundering solved. We'd better buy our designer black framed Blues Brothers sun glasses."

Ben's summary analysis brought a hooting response. "You said that we'd solve all three and we did it."

Chapter 23

Locals and tourists alike lined up to get in to buy a beer and whatever else was being sold from behind the neon lit bar that resembled a habituated disco on steroids. They were a younger crowd for the most part nonchalantly attired in the anti-establishment tourist uniform of sun-faded frayed denim and phony ponchos. They looked as if they had been chopped out of the same raw dough by the same cookie cutter. The music of 1960s American Band Stand hosted by the ever-young Dick Clark, now at an age almost past counting, wailed through the swinging doors in waves above the din of the wall-to-wall yelling and gyrating patrons inside.

On the street, small groups stood almost in drooping silence. Kaplanski was surprised at the lethargy of the drug-induced vacant young faces. He felt alone and alienated in the crowd and yet not anxious to retreat into his rented room with its neglected venetian blinds that magnified the mind-numbing repetition of the neurotic neon lights and incessant reverberating resonances of the impaired nightlife below.

He was tasting and breathing the stench of *las calles* and the barrio like a pollution seeping into him. There was no doubt in his mind that this would be his final undercover assignment. Being a member of the Musical Ride despite the horseshit, or being the only real Mountie amongst all the cardboard red-serge cut-outs on Parliament Hill was starting to appeal to him. He'd receive the same salary regardless. The salty air of the west coast was far more appealing, although he would have to mend several bridges before he'd apply for a transfer back to E Division. He would start today penning a note for Glen to deliver personally. For now, he'd just hum 'Rose Marie' under his breath.

Images of the 1936 black and white film with Jeanette McDonald and Nelson Eddie brought a subtle smile to his inner soul or at least to his outward demeanour. For whatever reason, it reminded him of his upbringing in the thriving metropolis of Drumheller in the Alberta bad lands, better known today for the renowned Royal Tyrrell Dinosaur Museum than the old homestead of Mister and Misses Kaplanski and their little boy Bill.

His mission on this final assignment had been relatively successful, reporting that there were Canadian entrepreneurs who had set up secret shell companies and accompanying bank accounts in the Grand Caymans, with the perception of impunity, where money was being laundered with direct and indirect deposits. Glen had complimented him the last time they had communicated. He was to report in one last time before returning home.

His mission was not necessarily to focus on the drug cartels. He just happened to be on their turf and in their backyards, which blanketed the entire region like a plague of starved locusts. In this sleaze of criminality, with which he was all too familiar, the two were inseparable. He would attempt to detach himself from the infectious malaise while he soaked up some last rays with what remained of his official unofficial vacation. His previous mission with the Toronto bike gang had been far more stressful, but that was behind him now, a lifetime away.

In his final communiqué to Glen, Kaplanski had reported that he had heard that a Russian hacker was working for the Cancun cartel. His IT skills were being used to e-infiltrate all competition and threats. Yes, the cartel had its vicious psychotic enforcers, like the late Don Miguel Garcia, to ensure compliance of the not so faithful mules and users, but the cartels had embraced the sophisticated e-world enthusiastically and were not constrained by fiscal budgets that were subject to claw-backs and annual audits.

***

"We will be landing in Toronto shortly, ladies and gentlemen. Please ensure that your table trays are in the upright position, your seat backs are in the full upright position, and all your baggage is stowed away in the bins about your head or beneath the seats in front of you."

Kaplanski breathed a sigh of relief. He was displaying a bronze tan, as were most of the other passengers who had not spent all their vacation hours sampling the numerous brands of Tequila in the shaded bars. Yet his vacation had not been completely void of its stressful moments. But that didn't seem to matter as he was home at last.

He had travelled light with just one checked bag. As he stood amongst the other passengers pushing and jockeying for position by the baggage carrousel, he heard a cryptic low vindictive whisper, "fuck you, cop." Simultaneously, he felt a searing pain in his back that penetrated into his heart. He fainted forward into the dizzying kaleidoscope of the empty carrousel. Screams faded away.

***

Surveillance CCTV recorded the murder, but the assailant could not be identified because he had been wearing a b-ball cap pulled down low over his eyes. Amidst all the confusion, the murderer calmly walked away with the assured stealth of a professional assassin. The stiletto ice pick that protruded from the entrance wound in Kaplanski's mid back had penetrated his heart.

"That's not like him to drop his guard," Glen reflected after having watched the recording several times. "He was better than that."

"He must have recognised the murderer," Ben commented. "I don't mean to make light of his murder, but it's classic Sherlock Holmes from the case of Silver Blaze."

"Explain," Glen responded, still dumbfounded by the circumstances.

"Regardless of what isn't there, however improbable, that must be the cause. It is essential to pay attention to what isn't there, not just what is there. That was the curious case of the silent dog in the disappearance of the racehorse, Silver Blaze, and the ostensible murder of its trainer. In that case, the absence of the barking of the dog was something that was all too easy to forget, Sherlock Holmes adroitly identified. We undervalue high probabilities and overvalue low probabilities."

"Excuse my thick head, Ben, but I need clarification," Glen mumbled. "Kaplanski did nothing at all."

"Not true," Ben replied. "Kaplanski did something. He chose not to respond in defence because he knew the assailant. We can never just assume that an absence means nothing."

"OK. I follow your logic this far," Glen confirmed. "But?"

"The absence of active rivalry reflects a decision not to fight. In this Sherlock Holmes case, the dog did not bark, it chose not to bark because it recognised the murderer. I conclude that, in all likelihood, Kaplanski recognised the murderer's voice. It is content – the known voice, within context – Toronto. The murderer had to have been a member of the Toronto bike gang. Else, Kaplanski would have swiftly turned around and confronted, engaged the assailant."

Glen smiled and inhaled a long, slow, deep breath, and extended his hand. "You are brilliant Constable Ben McLeod. That's where we start our search for the killer, in Kalpanski's personal notes and the file notes for that biker gang case."

"I'd like to be part of the investigative team."

"We will certainly use your analytical skills, Ben, but not in the day-to-day bull work, in the physical hunt for the killer. Your skills are far too valuable for just this singular case, albeit a very important case. We will train you and mould you into an invincible 21st century e-centurion. In the interim, I'm going to start reading Sir Arthur Conan Doyle and recommend that all my investigators become connoisseurs of Sherlock Holmes."

***

Corporal William Antonio Kaplanski was buried in the RCMP cemetery, Regina. Sue, Ben and their Detachment Commander, and Glen attended in addition to several of his Troop mates and an honour guard.

After the funeral service, Glen handed Sue an envelope with her name hand written. "Kaplanski sent this to me and asked that I give it to you personally."

As she read it, tears flowed down her cheeks.

They walked away from the gravesite and embraced in a muted moment.

Ben inquired with a compassionate tone, "all OK, partner?"

Silence paved their path further before Sue purposely bumped her shoulder against his. "All OK, partner. All OK."

Ben reviewed a message from Alejandra who swore with a passion that she had warned him about the Stalinist purge as soon as she heard. He re-analysed all the facts, especially the details of Kaplanski's murder. He wanted to believe her. It just wouldn't make logical sense not to. He replayed in his mind all the facts again, listened to his intuition, and re-analysed with the pragmatic precision of Sherlock Holmes. He concluded that perhaps it was that elementary, Watson.

Chapter 24

"One final debrief, folks," Glen quietly requested in a subdued fireside tone. "As a follow up to the Kalpanski case, the US Border patrol arrested the Russian hacker, Sergei Popov, illegally crossing into Texas. Sergei had agreed to assist them in return for immunity."

Sue shook her head in resigned repugnance at the thought of an immunity deal.

"Kaplanski had advised me that the Cancun cartel was employing a Russian hacker to e-infiltrate all competition. But Kaplanski wasn't aware that Sergei had hacked his cell phone and knew that Kaplanski was a cop from his text message and his cell phone calls. By happenstance, he was in his bank in the Grand Cayman when Kaplanski was there. That is where he picked up Kaplanski's e-messages on his scanner."

This time it was Ben who huffed in amazement at the coincidence of events.

"Sergei was being paid by Moscow and the Cancum cartel, and anyone else who had lots of cash for deposit into his account in the Grand Cayman Islands. Among his clients were bike gangs, specifically affiliates of the Toronto gang."

Sergei also revealed that Russians were hacking into the US Commerce Department. That was a national security issue that trumped all other criminal activities, including Kaplanski's murder. This is why he was granted immunity although he is currently under guarded house arrest.

"Let that be a lesson to all, that you use your own cell phone at your own peril and others in your network," Glen cautioned.

Ben immediately felt a lump in is throat. Had he compromised Alejandra's safety? He felt guilty for doubting her sincerity and veracity regarding her intelligence. He felt sick about possibly putting her life in danger.

"I have some news for both of you. It's unofficial. The Detachment Commander will make the formal announcement. Sue, you have been promoted to corporal and will be transferred to Sub-Division GIS."

"Congrats, partner," Ben beamed. "Let me be the first to shake your hand, Corporal Archer."

Glen reinforced his informal announcement. "We do not know who the corrupt sergeant is yet or the other member from the drug section who is on the take. We also do not yet know who the dirty crown prosecutor is, or the academic people and bank executive. So, it is imperative that you keep your radar up at all times and maintain all appearances of normalcy. This case was high profile so the knives may be still out there."

"I have some good news and some bad news, Ben," Glen spoke in his fatherly tone with Sue looking on. The good news, you will be attending the University of Calgary to complete a graduate degree in Spanish language and Spanish culture. Upon graduation, expect a posting with international associations that will take advantage of your multi-lingual skills. Like Sue, the Detachment Commander will officially inform you."

Sue bumped his shoulder and grinned. "Congrats to you too, partner."

"The bad news, Ben, the body of a Mexican female washed up on shore just south of Gibsons. It has been identified as Alejandra Martinez. I understand from speaking with Sue that you knew her. I am so very sorry to have to deliver this news."

Ben sat frozen in stunned silence. His head buzzed as the high shrill ringing in his left ear deafened him to what Sue was saying in support. After what appeared to be an eternity, he became aware of his surroundings, although words could not express his semi-conscious state.

It would not have been of any importance to Ben to know that her drowning had been reported to the two cartel agents arrested on the wharf, for onward communication to their respective cartel bosses.

"You have some vacation coming to you. You may want to return to Trail to visit with your family and relax as best you can before you start classes next month. It has been a mentally exhausting time for all but specifically for you. I'll keep in contact with you as will Sue."

***

Relic opened an envelope that had been taped to the window of the cabin door into his tugboat. In it was a plain Thank You card with the inscription, 'Met up with my friend at King's Bakery – very much appreciate your friendship at a time when I desperately needed a friend. Below is a gift in appreciation.' There was neither a return address nor a name. Relic looked down at a new automatic coffee pot. He smiled softly as he affectionately slid the card into the breast pocket of his flannel fisherman's shirt and mumbled, "Best in peace, mate. Best in peace."

Chapter 25

Ben took a seat in class. Living in residence at the University of Calgary would be convenient once the snow blanketed the campus. The underground tunnels that connected all the facilities would be a pleasant convenience when the scourge of old man winter froze everything above the terrain.

"Hello," a voice from the seat behind greeted him. "My name is Marcelle Santos. Do you have an interest in Spanish culture?"

His heart jumped. He gasped for a brief breath. "Yes. I once had a friend with Spanish background who inspired me from the first moment we met. She was a most elegant beautiful lady. She was warm, loving, sophisticated, cultured, and very romantic. Unfortunately, she drowned. I have grown to love the Spanish culture as much as I grew to love her."

"How wonderful. I sense that her memory is still a part of your life?"

Ben paused to wipe his eyes and clear his throat before responding. "Very much so. If she was here today, and we were not in a university classroom with everyone looking, I would hold her in my arms, make passionate love to her, and tell her how much I loved her. Unfortunately, we were from different worlds back then so we just tangoed."

"Do you tango?" Marcelle asked. "I have always wanted to learn. Perhaps you might teach me."

"Perhaps you can tutor me in Spanish in exchange for Tango lessons. The barter system seems to work well I understand."

Marcelle moved up and took an empty seat beside Ben. "Your friend, she sounds wonderful. Perhaps someday, you might tell me more about her."

"What are you doing after class, and for the rest of your life?" Ben asked with more emotion in his voice than he had ever experienced before.

"Would you like a banana and chocolate chip muffin?" Marcelle inquired. "I baked them fresh this morning. We could share after class. They are best fresh, you know, with freshly brewed coffee."

"I heard that fresh is best, especially in the morning with a caressing hug. I have a very special crocheted bag with my name embroidered on the flap that I could put them in. I only use the bag on equally special occasions."

"Here's my new phone number and email. It's a pseudonym, Ingrid, as in Ingrid Bergman. She starred in my very favourite Hollywood film, Casablanca."

"I also have a pseudonym. It's Bogie, after Humphrey Bogart who, as you will know, co-starred with Ingrid. Casablanca happens to be my favourite silver screen movie so much so that I have it downloaded. Perhaps you'd like to watch it with me sometime."